# JEMIMA SHORE INVESTIGATES

# JEMIMA SHORE INVESTIGATES

Thames Methuen
London

First published in Great Britain in 1983
by Methuen London Ltd
11 New Fetter Lane, London EC4P 4EE
in association with Thames Television International Ltd
149 Tottenham Court Road, London W1P 9LL

ISBN 0 423 00860 9

Printed in Great Britain by
Richard Clay (The Chaucer Press) Ltd,
Bungay, Suffolk

# Contents

# Investigating Jemima

Investigating Jemima Shore, biting the biter as it were, is not exactly an easy task since there is little co-operation to be expected from the person concerned: like most professional interviewers, Jemima hates being interviewed. Under the circumstances, we may as well start with her entry in *Who's Who*. (It's a recent inclusion, but 'long overdue' according to the *Woman's Guardian*.) The entry reads something like this:

SHORE, Jemima, television reporter; b. Bangalore 30th August. Only child of Col. Jeremy Shore and Eveline Phipps (both decd. Hong Kong). Educ: various schools abroad; Convent of the Blessed Eleanor, Churne, Sussex; Newnham College, Cambridge (1st class Hons. English). Writer and presenter of the Megalith Television series *Jemima Shore Investigates.* Awards include Golden Uranus (1979) for *The Pill – For or Against?*, also received NIFTA award (1980); Premio Donna Italiana (1981) for *The Poor and their Place*, also received NIFTA award (1982). Publications: *Jemima Shore Investigates ... Housing* (1978); *Jemima Shore Investigates ... Old Age* (1983).
    Recreations: Listening to music; talking to cats.
    Address: 27 Holland Park Mansions, London W14

or c/o Megalith Television, Megalithic House, London W1.

But that, the public would indignantly exclaim, is not the half of it! For one thing, who would recognise the glamorous Jemima Shore under the brief description of 'television reporter'? Although that, strictly speaking, is what she is, Jemima Shore *Investigator* is the title under which the public has taken her to its heart. She is billed as 'Investigator' because her series for Megalith concerns serious social issues; she approaches them in a way which is, to put it mildly, hard-hitting (although Jemima's deceptively gentle manner and her famously sweet smile tend to disarm her subjects – at least while they are answering her questions). But as a result of this billing, Jemima Shore is increasingly taken by the public for some kind of amateur sleuth, who will listen to their problems and then solve them. These problems include murder. And Jemima, because her middle name is Inquisitive (this remark is generally attributed to Jemima's aide at Megalith, the devoted but not uncritical Cherry), can never quite resist answering the appeals of the public . . .

Then there are no photographs in *Who's Who*, equally dissatisfying for the public, since Jemima Shore's appearance, ever elegant (oh, those Jean Muir clothes!) and at the same time ever sympathetic (there is nothing threatening or invulnerable about Jemima), is as much a part of her fame as her actual work. Jemima herself does not see it in quite that light, but she has learned to live with the situation, and she has certainly a thoroughly feminine enjoyment of the clothes (after all, she earns them).

In other ways, the public would be right: there is a great deal more to be known about Jemima Shore than is revealed by the sparse lines of *Who's Who*. Her Army

8

background is duly acknowledged: Jemima was born in India, a few weeks after Independence, when her father was still in the Indian Army; he transferred to the British Army later that year. As a result, Jemima's early childhood was spent travelling – or at any rate, rootless – in Army billets, in places as various as Germany, Northern Ireland, Cyprus and Aden.

It was when her father was stationed in Hong Kong (having reached the rank of Colonel) that he was killed, together with Jemima's mother in a car crash. That left Jemima at the age of just on eighteen bereft of all family ties, but it also meant that she was independent of family obligations. This independence gained a further dimension in that Jemima inherited at this point, from her parents' life insurance, enough money to buy the large, light, balcony flat, overlooking Holland Park, in which she still lives. That apart, Jemima is secretly proud of making her way in the world without benefit of family connections. Nor does she envy her friends their massive family networks: she, after all, has the wonderful privilege of choosing her own network.

*Who's Who* also does not state one very important fact about Jemima's background, which is that she first adored her father, but then gradually came to see through him. Jeremy Shore was the ideal father when Jemima was a little girl: handsome, generous and dashing (Jemima gets her looks from her father). What Jemima did not realise then, and even now cannot contemplate without a pang, was that Colonel Shore shared his handsome person with an increasing number of grateful members of the female sex as the years went by. As for her mother, Mrs Shore never stopped loving her errant husband – and thus never stopped suffering.

It is nevertheless from poor down-trodden Eveline Shore that Jemima gets her intelligence; if only Eveline Shore had been able to use her brain for something other than being Colonel Shore's dowdy little wife! She did give Jemima a lot of discreet encouragement where her education was concerned, whilst carefully assuring her husband that Jemima was not being turned into an unattractive blue-stocking of the sort he would be ashamed to own as a daughter. Since Colonel Shore was not a notably successful soldier – perhaps philandering was not conducive to a brilliant career – Mrs Shore secretly began to pin her hopes upon her daughter. All the same, the fact that Jemima has remained unmarried probably springs deep down from a determination that *she* is never going to repeat her mother's life story, never going to find herself the adoring partner of an unfaithful husband, however handsome.

As for Jemima's educational record, that brief entry concerning the Convent of the Blessed Eleanor at Churne scarcely does justice to the impact which a Catholic convent, Catholic nuns and Catholic girls made upon the little Protestant girl, sent there first as a day-girl when her father was posted near Churne, later as a boarder. It was indeed a murder at the Convent of the Blessed Eleanor which brought about Jemima's first proper investigation (see *Quiet as a Nun*). Although not a Catholic herself – her Nonconformist blood rebels – she respected, and continues to respect, the nuns. She also keeps up with at least one friend from her convent days, Lady Miranda, currently Clay (Miranda has already been married twice, and now the Clay marriage is said to be on the rocks). But there is more to Miranda than her chaotic private life would indicate: after all she runs a chain of dress shops with almost as much efficiency as Jemima runs her programme. In both cases, Jemima puts it down to their early training: convent girls, she says, can run anything.

At Cambridge Jemima got a starred First in English (she modestly refrains from noting the star in *Who's Who*) and after that worked briefly for a publisher before turning to the new world of television, in which she rapidly rose. From Cambridge days Jemima derived another close woman friend, Becky Robertson; they also both went into television at the same moment. Nowadays, Becky is married with a child: Helen, Jemima's treasured god-daughter. Now a social worker, she provides quite a lot of material for Jemima's programmes. Becky is not only admirable and committed, she's also a good friend – but in certain moods it must be admitted that it is still Miranda that Jemima wants to call.

Jemima is also extremely close to her aide at Megalith, Cherry Bronson, she whose curves are the toast of Megalithic House and have earned her the nickname of Flowering Cherry. But the closest woman in Jemima's life in some ways is her daily, Mrs Bancroft, otherwise known as Mrs B, who is as passionately in love with Jemima as any member of the public. Where would Jemima be without Mrs B? It's a question asked frequently by Mrs B herself – for Mrs B is a great communicator – even if Jemima does not always answer. Who would water the precious plants on Jemima's balcony and in the flat? Above all, who would look after her cat? There is always a cat in Jemima's life. The current cat, called Midnight, is wayward and beautiful. He succeeds Tiger, who came into her life as a result of an investigation (see *A Splash of Red*), directly following the death of her beloved tabby Colette. Jemima hopes there will always be Mrs B in her life as well; even when Mrs B's cheerful analysis of last night's viewing on television is particularly prolonged, she still loves her. Really, Mrs B should be featured in *Who's Who* along with the other details of Jemima's life, as Jemima's true support-system.

There's always a man in Jemima's life too, although she's extremely secretive about it. As a free woman – in the legal sense as well as every other – she considers it nobody's business but her own. This is not, however, the line taken by Mrs B who, though the soul of discretion where the outside world is concerned, is possibly even more thrilled by Jemima's rich private life than Jemima is herself. When the odd guest stops over in Jemima's Holland Park flat and is still there for a late breakfast – something she does not necessarily encourage – Jemima reflects wryly: 'Well, at least Mrs B will be pleased.' However, since Jemima persists in playing these particular cards very close to her chest, no one, including Mrs B, can be *absolutely* sure which relationships have been genuinely important to her. After all, as well as lovers, Jemima has plenty of male friends who (we assume) are no more to her than that.

There's Jamie Grand for example – a powerful literary figure these days. He's the editor of *Literature* and also reviews plays: his collected pieces, *Grand Occasions*, *Volumes One*, *Two* and *Three* so far, are often compared to Agate's *Ego* series. Jamie generally has at least one very young and very pretty blonde in tow, but he will always escort Jemima to a first night, particularly since they share similar theatrical tastes. Both loathe George Bernard Shaw for example (Jemima thinks the name is spelt wrong, for a start). Then there's Guthrie Carlyle at Megalith Television, another friend and ally of long standing.

Jemima's relationship with the handsome Labour MP Tom Amyas, on the other hand, was undeniably more intimate. But that was one affair about which Jemima was very discreet indeed, despite its length, because Tom Amyas was and is married to an extremely possessive wife (Tom's wife Carrie Amyas is one person Jemima cannot bring herself to be charitable about), to say nothing of the danger to the constituency. Even Mrs B was never *quite* sure about that one: she did try passing flattering remarks whenever Tom Amyas appeared on television, but Jemima never rose to the bait.

Possibly that was the most important relationship in Jemima's life – so far. Or perhaps a strange tragic episode in Scotland on holiday (see *The Wild Island*) was the one which marked her; it involved a certain Colonel Henry Beauregard, who reminded her just a little of her father. Since, however, Jemima has never since mentioned Colonel Henry's name to anyone – not even to Miranda (too indiscreet) or to Becky (too disapproving on class grounds) – it is impossible to be certain.

Where professional relationships are concerned, first and foremost there's Pompey: Detective Chief Inspector Portsmouth of the Yard. Jemima first encountered him on a television programme when Pompey was issuing an appeal about a missing child. A friendship was struck up, based on the odd drink, the odd chat, the odd consultation about each other's work; on at least one occasion Jemima has managed to solve a mystery for Pompey, and *vice versa*.

Then of course there's Cy Fredericks of Megalith Television, to whom Jemima owes a lot, although not quite as much as Cy, in what may be termed his megalithic mood, thinks she does. Jemima and Cy have a long-standing tradition of sparring over what sort of programmes Jemima should make. Sometimes Jemima wins, if only because Cy's taste for what he asserts to be business travel gives her frequent openings. Sometimes

Cy does — as when he obliged Jemima to investigate theatrical festivals nationwide for murky internal reasons still unclear — was there a boardroom struggle somewhere along the line? Anyway the result on that occasion (see *Cool Repentance*) was a disaster for Megalith in financial terms, so perhaps it was victory for Jemima after all.

Jemima's recreations at least are accurately listed in *Who's Who* — as far as they go: as well as talking to cats, she does indeed like listening to music, Mozart being the prime favourite (*Don Giovanni* is her favourite opera), although she also likes classical jazz. Many things, however, are omitted, including the fact that Jemima likes to drive her own car fast (the latest is a white Mercedes sports car). In a more passive way, she adores receiving flowers, which should be white for preference: where Jemima is concerned, a quantity of white roses will get you anywhere — well, almost anywhere. Cherry has been known to tip off people about this, when she favours their suit, professional or otherwise. Just as she warns her favourites that Jemima's habitual drink is white wine: champagne is a treat, but Jemima never touches spirits or liqueurs, and thinks sherry should be abolished.

Most crucial of all the omissions among Jemima's recreations is her passion for lying in the bath for as long as possible, and then just a bit longer. She collects bath essences, the smell of tuberose or gardenia or wild hyacinth wafting in the air from the bathroom being a familiar greeting to Mrs B when she arrives at the flat.

But then, as Jemima firmly announces when teased about this passion, 'I think in the bath.'

It is often while Jemima is lying in one of her baths, that the telephone rings, and an unknown voice begins:

'Is that Jemima Shore Investigator? You don't know me, but I've seen you on television so I feel *I* know *you*. Listen, I need your help . . .'

That is one appeal Jemima the Inquisitive can never reject . . . So the next investigation begins . . .

# The Case of the Dancing Duchess

The red ON-AIR light on the studio wall went out. Another edition of *Jemima Shore Investigates* was over. The audience began to shuffle out, and their excited chatter was joined by the studio crew. The set was already being dismantled around her as Jemima leant back in her presenter's chair. She stretched her arms out taut behind her, like her favourite animals cats, after a long sleep in front of a fire. Jemima Shore, however, had certainly not been relaxing for the past hour. As Megalith's star presenter, hosting her own enormously popular show, she examined an important social topic each week. Tonight's programme was the first one of the autumn season after the summer break, and, naturally, Jemima was even more concerned than usual that this one was a success. It was important that each series got off to a good start.

The spectacular success and popularity of the show, Jemima believed (and not immodestly), came from her being more than just a front person. She wasn't just wheeled on as a mouthpiece, but was always personally involved with the background research and editorial decision-making. Usually, Jemima herself suggested the subject for the programme.

'Great show, Jem,' said one of the sound crew, as he unclipped the small radio-mike from the front of her dress. 'It's great you're back. Terrif.'

'Thanks, Pete.' Jemima smiled at him. It *was* good to be back making programmes again. She never realised just how much she missed working until she started up again.

Jemima stood up and picked her way carefully out across the studio floor, stepping over cables and between the large studio cameras on their pedestals. She paused occasionally to chat with the crew while they cleared away the equipment. Unlike some stars, Jemima was just as popular with the people she worked with as with the public.

Leaving the studio through the double doors that kept the outside world out during a show, Jemima made her way to the make-up department. Megalith sometimes seemed to consist of interminable corridors decorated with stills from its shows, past and present. And there she was, hanging next to the entrance to make-up – one of the nation's most famous faces, staring out from a poster advertising the new series: 'What will Jemima Shore Investigate this week?'

Jemima sat herself down in front of the unflattering make-up mirror. The face it reflected was not one of classic beauty, but it showed a particular cool, English intelligence. No matter how knotted up she was inside, Jemima always gave the impression of serene poise externally. Even in the toughest interviews, she looked relaxed and in control, yet never unfeminine. Jemima was aware – slightly cynically, but certainly in good humour – that her success came in part from the fact that men fancied her, but women admired her. People confided in Jemima, and she found she could ask all sorts of questions that male journalists would find it difficult to get away with. But her success also depended on a great deal of hard work: to have become such a success while she was still only in her mid-thirties was an indication of Jemima's skill, talent and determination.

She took some cotton-wool balls from the box on the top in front of her and began to remove her make-up. It had gone rather well, she mused, thinking back on the evening's programme. It was always difficult to know how to start off a new series, but this programme had seemed to work. 'Justifiable homicide' was the subject for the programme. It had most of the ingredients that were said to be necessary for a best-selling novel – violence and class, at least, if overtly no sex. The star had been not the predictable reformed psychopath or worthy do-gooder, although she had included lawyers in force, but an elderly duchess.

Getting the Duchess of Montfort to appear on the programme had been a considerable coup. Jemima had needed all her most persuasive charm, and was surprised that the Duchess had agreed to talk about the case on television. The case had been all over the papers, a *cause célèbre* and much-discussed scandal for several days, if not weeks – anyway, a long time in Fleet Street. But then it is not every day that an elderly dowager duchess fires a shotgun into an intruder and kills him – even on the grounds of self-defence.

She seemed to have no conscience about having killed a man, and when asked if she believed in the death penalty for murder, she replied, looking Jemima straight in the eye, 'A death deserves a death.' At that moment in the programme, Jemima knew millions of viewers would be riveted. Never mind the Duchess seemed to show no remorse for the legal beagles boring on about the niceties of the law – here was someone who had actually killed a person, admitted it, and felt no guilt. What's more, Jemima gathered she had the backing of the law in what she had done.

Jemima had to admit it herself: *she* was personally intrigued by the Duchess of Montfort. Beneath that old-world charm, she sensed a personality as soft as icy steel. Not many sixty-five-year-olds could fill a burglar with bullets with no apparent difficulty. So when the Duchess invited her back for drinks at her town house, Jemima accepted with enthusiasm. She was looking forward to talking to her further – and the house was the scene of the killing. Jemima Shore Investigator was not going to miss an opportunity like that. Further, the Duchess was no ordinary aristocrat: she had started life in the back row of the chorus. Jemima wanted to chat to her about the early days in the theatre. Who knew: she might be able to find a new angle for the programme on theatre she had always had a yearning to do.

Jemima's thoughts on how to get the Duchess to open up and talk to her about her past were interrupted by the arrival of Cherry, her jolly personal assistant. Cherry was more than a glorified secretary – in fact, Jemima sometimes wondered how on earth she woud survive without Cherry to organise her life for her. Not only did Cherry know the whole process of programme-making inside out, but she also understood exactly how Jemima thought and operated. Indeed, Cherry often bore the brunt of translating Jemima's ideas into a do-able form. She was also expert at protecting Jemima and keeping the world at bay when Jemima's precious privacy was being threatened.

Mentally and physically, however, the two girls could not have been more unlike. This was probably why they worked so well together. Sometimes Jemima felt more like a wise older sister than boss to the pert and perky Cherry, whose main loves in life were food and men though not necessarily in that order. Jemima was one of those enviable people who can eat as much as they like and never put on an ounce in weight. Jemima had no problems in maintaining her slim figure; Cherry seemed to be fighting a perpetual battle of the bulge. Cherry had just returned from holiday in Paris, where she had done a Cordon Bleu course. When she failed in her pursuit of older men, Cherry found solace in cooking the most elaborate and delicious meals.

'So! Who's new then?' asked Cherry, pointing to an enormous (and therefore slightly vulgar) bouquet of white roses that had been delivered to Jemima whilst she was putting the finishing touches to her street make-up. Jemima grimaced. Leo Squire, Megalith Television's new chat-show host was concentrating on chatting her up. He was pursuing Jemima with a relentless determination – but singular lack of imagination: after all, he had taken the trouble to find out her favourite flowers – and then mis-judged how to use that knowledge. What little attraction he might initially have had for Jemima was soon over-ridden by his obvious approach. He was really much more Cherry's type, Jemima thought, as she caught a flicker of jealousy register on her PA's face.

'I don't think he has ever heard the word No,' said Jemima. 'He's waiting upstairs in the bar, for dinner after the show, if you fancy trying your chances with him.'

'You're standing him up then?' Cherry gasped, appalled at Jemima's cavalier attitude to Leo, whom she considered the most attractive man at Megalith.

'It's not as if he even asked me,' Jemima retorted tartly. 'He assumed he just had to click his fingers and I'd come running. Anyway, I already have a date for this evening – with the Duchess, I better say, before your mind starts working overtime.'

Cherry looked quizzically at Jemima. 'I thought she seemed a tough old bird. Not someone to spend a fun-packed evening with. I can just see her emptying two barrels of a shotgun into an intruder.'

'He did pull a Luger on her,' Jemima commented, as she brushed her glossy reddy-gold hair.

'Yeah, but that comes naturally to the upper classes, after years of practice mutilating serfs.'

Jemima smiled. Cherry's class allegiances were pretty transparent. 'Not in her case, Cherry. Remember, the Duchess was a show-girl.'

Cherry raised an eyebrow. 'So that's why you're having drinks with her? To glean some more anecdotes for your "wicked women of the stage" idea?'

'That, and a desire to see the site of one of the sensations of the Fleet Street year.'

'I didn't think you were a voyeur,' said Cherry cheekily.

'Here, have these! A compensation present if you don't succeed with Leo Squire!' Jemima picked up the bouquet of flowers and flung them at Cherry, who caught them with an ill grace, but inwardly supposing that cast-off flowers were marginally better than cast-off men.

'Come on. Cheer up! Tell me some more about your Paris jaunts while I sign my letters. I must then drive the Duchess home.'

Jemima soon cleared her desk and, having collected the Duchess from Megalith's hospitality suite, drove her home. Jemima's white open-top Mercedes drew up outside the Duchess's stucco Belgravia home. The Duchess lived in one of those wide, quiet London streets that oozed money. None of the vast four-storeyed houses in this street had been sub-divided into flats. They were all still separate family houses. The Duchess's house was on the corner of the elegant white terrace, facing a classically styled parish church on the other side of the road. Maybe, one day, thought Jemima, I'll be able to afford to buy a house like this. Probably not. In truth, she told herself, she enjoyed her bachelor-girl independence, and was perfectly content with her Holland Park flat.

Jemima helped the Duchess out from the low-slung car, but her offers of assistance were brushed aside as she tried to hold her arm while climbing the steps up to the front door. Before the door was open, the two women were assailed by the excited sound of barking. The front door was opened by the tall and dignified figure of Tupper, the butler, who was brushed aside by a frisky, glossy-haired red setter.

'Be quiet Mason,' the Duchess ordered as they entered the hallway. 'One of the late Duke's guard dogs. Fortnum died.'

Jemima smiled wryly and looked round the vast hallway. Stretching up ahead of her was an imposing marble staircase. The marble floor of the hall was partly covered by some extremely beautiful and antique-looking Persian rugs. The walls were covered with what looked like the Montfort family history in pictures – mainly vast and dull brown in colour. The centre-piece of the room, however, was a huge, sparkling, shimmering chandelier.

'Tupper!' admonished the Duchess sharply as Tupper ogled Jemima. 'Tupper is a great enthusiast of the television,' she remarked.

'Yes indeed, Ma'am. Your show is one of my favourites. Yours and Leo Squire's. I think he is very talented.'

'So does he,' said Jemima dryly.

'I must say, I thought tonight's programme excellent, Miss Shore – and, of course, Your Grace. Very thought-provoking.'

'It is all over now, Tupper,' the Duchess snapped. 'That's the main thing. I have been vindicated by the High Court, and now by the media.' She was getting very impatient. Tupper was so overcome with the excitement of meeting Jemima Shore in real life, that he had failed to take the Duchess's cape. Jemima was accustomed to this gawking by now, but was surprised to find it in someone like a butler. In an attempt to cover the awkwardness, Jemima admired the garment.

'Designed it myself, my dear, and had it run up by a little woman I know. It is impossible to buy anything ready-made these days that actually keeps one dry. Anyway, do come upstairs and have some champagne – the late Duke kept a rather decent cellar.'

'My favourite drink, Duchess,' said Jemima, as indeed it was. Jemima could not abide drinking spirits, and stuck to white wine whenever she was drinking.

Jemima followed the Duchess up the stairs and into her drawing room on the first floor. This was a large room running the full width of the house. Definitely a woman's room, it contrasted sharply with the entrance-hall. It was crammed with pretty sofas and chairs in delicate pretty pink tones. There were numerous small side tables covered with photographs and small china figurines. Over the fireplace hung a large oil painting of the Duchess, done – judging from her clothes – in the first flush of post-war euphoria, with the New Look. Pride of place, however, went to a bronze statuette of a dancer. Instinctively, Jemima went up to admire it.

'Do you like it?' asked the Duchess.

'Why, it's beautiful!' exclaimed Jemima. 'You can feel the movement in it. There is so much life in it, so much youth.' She was quite entranced by the charming object.

'That is me, my dear. When I was Eloise Claire, the dancer.' Jemima must have looked surprised for a moment, for the Duchess continued, 'Don't worry. I'm not ashamed of my origins. In fact, I'm rather proud of what I've done with my life. I'm proud of my achievements as Eloise Claire, and I'm proud of my achievements as the Duchess of Montfort. Both careers, you may be surprised to hear, require very much the same qualities.'

'Which are . . .?' inquired Jemima.

'I must say, that sounds rather like one of your television questions, Miss Shore.'

'Oh . . .! I'm sorry,' apologised Jemima. 'I didn't mean to sound rude. And please call me "Jemima", not "Miss Shore". It is so formal. Do please believe me – I am genuinely interested in the theatre.'

The Duchess turned to Jemima. 'Now that's a fatal thing to say to an old trouper like myself.' The Duchess was beginning to mellow. The famous Jemima Shore magic with people was beginning to work. The Duchess indicated that Jemima should sit on the sofa facing the huge marble fireplace. Jemima was pleased to see a fire blazing away. Next to having a bath, there was nothing more relaxing, she thought, than sitting in front of her own small open fire. Her best thoughts came to her when she was lying in her Victorian bath tub, but watching the red glow of a real fire provided hours of comfort when she was alone in her flat. Mason evidently agreed with her, because he had stretched himself out in front of the fire by the elaborate brass fender. Jemima sat down on the sofa, but, although decorative, it turned out to be more conducive to correct posture than to comfort.

The Duchess crossed the room and picked up a large leather-bound album from a walnut occasional table, and came to sit next to Jemima on the sofa. 'My theatrical scrapbook,' the Duchess needlessly explained. Jemima was fascinated.

Meanwhile, Tupper had fetched the champagne – a good vintage, Jemima was pleased to see. He served the drink in the old-fashioned shallow Edwardian champagne glasses. These suited the room, with the delicacy of their greenish glass and slender fluted stems.

Both women sipped the wine, but were far more interested in the Duchess's scrapbook. A whole era, past and never to return, came alive as the Duchess turned the pages. The same unflinching eyes stared out from the pictures of the young Eloise Claire as had gazed at Jemima earlier that evening. The Duchess had been one of C. B. Cochrane's Young Ladies, and from the back chorus rose to become a solo artist. The scrapbook was full of programmes and photographs charting the era when theatrical verve was at its height. 'That's me singing "Hanging Around for You" in "Joybells".' The Duchess pointed at a photo of a beautiful young girl posed on her own with a slightly saucy hat on.

'"Jumblesale", at the Vaudeville – that was my last performance,' said the Duchess, as she snapped the scrapbook shut. 'I had met the Duke before the show opened, during another revue, and when it closed I married him, and my life and world altered completely. It was goodbye to the world of theatre. Though I must say that life on the stage prepares one for the aristocracy better than public school seems to. I taught the Duke everything about how to behave at ceremonial occasions. I gave him a sense of theatre.'

'You have no regrets about leaving the stage?' inquired Jemima.

'Not about leaving the stage.' The Duchess sighed and murmured, 'I do have regrets that there is no one to come after me. Don't get me wrong, Miss Shore . . . Jemima, the Duke and I were very happy – perfectly content – but now he is dead and I'm on my own, the sadness is that when I go there will be no one to inherit. I don't mind about the title – there is an heir in New

Zealand. But I'd like to leave something to someone close to me — to help someone on their way. I have been poor, and I know what money can mean. As I get older, I would like to find someone, someone related to me, someone . . .' The Duchess broke off, and for the first time, Jemima saw a crack in her composure. Staring straight in front of her, directly into the fire, the Duchess seemed lost in a reverie. Jemima did not wish to intrude and decided it was time to go.

'How ungracious of me,' said the Duchess, starting up as if she had been asleep.

'I must go. Though I'd love to come back and talk some more about your early life on the stage. That is if you don't think me too presumptuous.' Jemima slowly rose from the sofa.

'Any time, my dear. Any time. You would be most welcome. I'll call Tupper to see you out.' The frail old lady walked across from the sofa to the bell push, on the wall next to the fireplace. She pushed the bell assertively, and wandered to the large windows, draped with long dark-rose velvet curtains. She parted them and slowly looked out over the street. 'Good heavens. It's raining.' Rain was pouring down outside; one could see huge puddles collecting on the pavements. Jemima had come without a coat. By this time Tupper had arrived, and was ordered to fetch the Duchess' cape. Even in the short walk from the front door to her car, which was only parked a few yards down the street, Jemima's elegant cream suit would have been ruined.

Jemima thanked the Duchess for her kind offer, and promised to return the garment on her way into work the following day. She wrapped herself up in the cape which Tupper proffered her, and said her goodnights.

She really meant to talk further with the Duchess; there was a wealth of information there. Maybe the

Duchess could be persuaded to write her memoirs. What a fascinating life, thought Jemima, as she carefully made her way down the slippery front steps. High heels were an essential Jemima hall-mark, but she would look pretty silly if she slipped and had to spend the rest of the series in a plaster cast.

Her thoughts returned to the Duchess. Quite a woman – from a two up, two down in Deptford, to a baronial Scottish castle and a London mansion. No mean feat.

Jemima had by now reached the bottom of the steps, and was about to make the dash through the rain to her car when a shot rang out.

'Murderer! Murderer!' An hysterical high-pitched male voice cried out through the rain.

Jemima froze, considering if and where to dive for cover, but before she had time to decide, an elderly white-haired gentleman, dressed in an old-fashioned evening suit, was bowing to her.

'Eloise, I'm so sorry . . .' the old man began, but then started back in surprise. 'But you're *not* Eloise. Miss Shore! Miss Jemima Shore. *Enchanté*. My name is Freddie Prideaux: I do apologise for my brother's behaviour.' That seemed rather an inadequate remark considering she had just been shot at, but cowering in the church doorway on the other side of the street was a smaller, fatter man, of about the same age as Freddie. 'My brother Cecil,' the first explained.

A sob came from Cecil, and he staggered across the street to Jemima and Freddie, who were getting increasingly bedraggled in the rain. Jemima could smell the reek of whisky from Cecil as he approached. She began to regain her poise. Two geriatrics, one a drunk verging on hysteria, did not after all seem to pose a great threat to her.

'I thought you were Eloise,' Cecil said in way of explanation. He was shaking all over, his hands twitching. Fortunately, Freddie had knocked the gun from his brother's hand, and had put it in his pocket, out of reach.

'And why were you trying to kill the Duchess?'

'I was afraid you might ask that, Miss Shore.' Jemima took it for granted by now that people would instantly recognise her. However, she was not used to being shot at. Her natural curiosity was now fully aroused. After all, as Cherry put it, her middle name was 'Inquisitive'. Her antennae knew she was on to a good story: ATTEMPTED MURDER OF TV STAR OUTSIDE DUCHESS'S HOUSE. This had the makings of an even better story than the Duchess's one earlier that evening. Apart from her professional interest, Jemima was also understandably interested to know why someone had tried to kill her, even if by mistake.

Cecil was in no fit state to talk out in the street. They had to move somewhere. It had begun to rain even harder. There would be no welcome in the Duchess's house for someone who had intended to kill her on her own doorstep. There was no alternative: if Jemima wanted to find out more about the attempted killing, she would have to drive the brothers home.

It was a tight squeeze in Jemima's Mercedes sports car. Freddie sat virtually doubled up in the back, and Cecil was firmly strapped into the passenger seat, with both windows open in a hope that fresh, cold air would sober him up on his way home. Jemima was a good driver, and ignored the drunken outbursts from Cecil next to her and the repeated apologies coming from Freddie behind, concentrating on getting to their destination.

The Prideaux brothers lived in one of those large Edwardian mansion blocks near the Marylebone Road, now on their way up again in the world. Jemima felt that the brothers, however, were going the other way. Initially, when they moved in, between the Wars, it would have been a fashionable address, but it had declined during the 'fifties and 'sixties. She imagined they had lived here for years on a fixed peppercorn rent.

Jemima felt she was going to be overcome by Cecil's whisky fumes as the three travelled up in the creaky, antiquated lift to the top floor, where the Prideaux flat was situated. Freddie heaved the metal folding doors open, and directed Jemima down a narrow corridor painted a gloomy green. He opened the front door and showed Jemima into the living room, while he despatched Cecil to bed to sober up.

Jemima looked round the brothers' living room with interest. Obviously a theatrical pair, the walls were covered with playbills and theatre posters, but in places there were brown patches where there had been pictures which had been recently taken down. Had they been sold, Jemima wondered. The predominant feeling was one of fading gentility alongside a slight prissy tidiness. Everything had once been ever so smart, but that was now many years ago. However there was a well-loved, cared-for feel to the place which Jemima liked. The brothers enjoyed their home. Pride of place was given to a grand piano which gleamed by the window. Having glanced at the theatrical memorabilia on the walls, Jemima sat down in a large and comfortable high-winged armchair, next to a coffee table covered with books.

'Let me make you one of my specialities,' said Freddie as he entered the room, moving over to a well-stocked drinks tray. Although the other brother was obviously the one with a drink problem, Freddie was probably in need of a settling drink himself. In fact, Jemima realised, she could also do with one. Being shot at, she decided, was somewhat *un*settling.

'A Prideaux Heartfonder,' said Freddie, pouring the contents of a number of bottles into a chrome cocktail shaker. 'My own little invention. Much the best thing I ever composed. Much better than any of those ditties Cecil and I used to do in revue.'

'Heartfonder?' smiled Jemima. She didn't believe that she was now going to be propositioned by a geriatric. She couldn't help but warm to this charming ana-chronism of a man. His obvious dismay at what his brother had done to Jemima, and his old-fashioned good manners, endeared him to her.

'Because it's full of absinthe,' said Freddie, 'which as you know . . .'

'. . . makes the heart grow fonder,' laughed Jemima, finishing off the sentence.

'A bright as well as charming girl,' purred Freddie. 'I'm afraid I spent most of my youth with girls from the chorus, having dinner at the Ivy. They were charming, but not what one would call over-bright.'

'Thank you so much, but I'm afraid I'm extremely boring and usually only drink wine,' said Jemima.

'But it's got wine in it, my dear – a whole drop, I promise you.' Freddie pressed his concoction on Jemima, so that she couldn't have the ill grace to refuse. She took a sip and gasped: it stung the back of her throat.

'It's very . . .'

'Yes, isn't it. I'm sorry I've been babbling. I've fre-quently had to apologise for my brother's behaviour before, but never to someone he tried to kill. I'm not sure what the correct form is.'

'Well, thank goodness you arrived in the nick of time and knocked the gun out of his hand. How did you know what was happening?' inquired Jemima.

'I came home from a first night at the Royal Court — I still believe in keeping up appearances. Difficult, don't y'know, on a fixed income. I don't know why I bother, though — tonight there were no words with more than four letters, and come to that, few with less. Here, look at this. I found this when I arrived home from the theatre.' He handed Jemima a note which in Freddie's heyday would have been known as a *billet doux*.

Jemima read: 'I have to do it, Freddie. I must avenge poor Kenneth's foul and unnatural murder.' Rather melodramatic, thought Jemima and asked, 'Poor Kenneth?'

'Well you see, Kenneth was Cecil's little boy,' said Freddie. Kenneth turned out to have been hardly a boy, at sixty-three, but that was young to the two octogenerians. It transpired that Kenneth was Kenneth Exton, the Duchess's intruder, and that Cecil believed that Kenneth was trying to blackmail her, which was the cause for his death.

'She murdered him,' came a cry from the doorway and, even drunker, Cecil lurched across the room to sit down opposite Jemima and Freddie. 'She murdered him, Miss Shore, and it would all be over now if you hadn't borrowed her cape. I would have shot her just as she shot dear Kenneth and then I would have shot myself and that would have been the end of it.'

Jemima felt pity for this frail wreck of a man, an aged alcoholic homosexual for whom life now held nothing. Cecil clasped his head in his hands and let out a little howl of despair.

'I feel so frightfully embarrassed,' stammered Cecil to Jemima. He turned to Freddie and demanded another drink.

'You've already had . . .'

'Oh, shut up!' rejoined Cecil.

Freddie glanced apologetically at Jemima, and slowly got up to pour his brother another whisky. Cecil blew his nose and rubbed his hands up and down across the tops of his legs. Jemima looked at the veined face and faded bloodshot blue eyes of a lush, and spoke to Cecil. 'Listen, if you really believe that the Duchess murdered Kenneth, then that's something that needs proper investigation.'

'It's had what's called a proper investigation,' retorted Cecil. 'In the courts. What happens? She buys the best defence lawyer in the country and goes scot free – no stain on her character and what's more, a pat on the back from the judge for being a "good citizen".'

'That doesn't mean you can take the law into your own hands,' answered Jemima. Cecil looked at her bitterly.

'Why not? What's the law ever done for me? For most of my life it's told me that everything I feel, that just being my natural self, is illegal. She can murder people and . . .'

'You've got to have proof, Cecil, before you can accuse her of murder, and in any case, she can't be tried twice for the same crime,' Jemima interrupted. However, all her instincts were now aroused. There was something about Cecil. There was more here than the grief of a rambling old man, albeit given to melodrama – there was something that made her feel he was telling the truth, and she would get to the bottom of it. It was very late by now, and Cecil had had far too much drink for a constructive talk, but Jemima agreed to return the following day and review the situation with the two brothers.

Jemima popped round to the Prideaux flat during the lunch hour the next day. The flat was not very far from Megalithic House. Cecil had sobered up, and it was he who let Jemima into the apartment. When sober, he shared some of his brother's old-world charm, and made Jemima smile as they searched through the contents of Kenneth's room.

'Your presence here would have been most inappropriate when I was young. Unchaperoned, in a gentleman's bedroom ... Tut, tut! You'd have been considered a fallen woman.'

'Not with you, surely,' Jemima joked.

'Oh yes. Any man with a woman. Yes. A man and a man, no, and a woman and woman, no. Things are very different now. Everyone has dirty minds.'

'Yes, I'm afraid Freud has a lot to answer for,' replied Jemima, as she looked through another drawer in the chest of drawers. They were searching for some clue to Kenneth's visit to the Duchess.

'Was the Duchess Kenneth's first victim?'

Cecil shook his head forlornly. 'K ... – you know it still hurts to speak his name ... No, K ... K ... Kenneth,' he stuttered, 'would try any money-making venture as long as it was illegal.' Jemima learnt that Kenneth Exton had been an illegitimate child, fostered at birth, and had spent his boyhood in and out of children's homes. As a youth he had got into trouble with petty larceny, and had been in and out of prison ever since. Jemima could see nothing very appealing in the spiv-like character of the photos that Cecil showed her, but then the heart was a strange thing.

'Have you ever loved someone totally unsuitable?' asked Cecil. Jemima looked at him gently. 'Yes, yes, I have.' And then she pressed on, wanting not to discuss emotional matters, but to discover as much as she could about Kenneth, so that there might be some lead. 'What were Kenneth's blackmailing methods? Would he have written to the Duchess?'

'Oh no,' interrupted Cecil. 'I'm afraid he wasn't at all educated. He was barely literate. He would have phoned and hinted at what he knew. He once told me about blackmail. "Feed it slowly," he said. "Make them squirm." He took pleasure in hurting people, you see.' Cecil broke off. Jemima pressed on; with so little to go on, she needed as much information about Kenneth as she could gain. 'So, he would have rung the Duchess asking for money?'

'Yes, she must have invited him to the flat. He went round, and there she was waiting ready for him with her shotgun.'

'You're only guessing,' interjected Jemima.

'No, I know,' snapped Cecil. 'Kenneth was a criminal, but he was never violent. He never used a gun. I can swear to that – I had to go out and obtain the one I tried to use on you.'

'In that case,' said Jemima, cutting him short, 'the solution lies in finding out what he was blackmailing the Duchess with. If we discover that we might be on our way.'

Cecil looked at her bleakly. 'Blackmailers don't file their material, do they? We have been through all the stuff here and there's nothing. I do wish you'd never come on the scene, Miss Shore.' At this point Cecil was on the verge of breaking down again, when they were fortunately interrupted by Freddie, announcing that lunch was ready.

Cecil drank continuously throughout lunch, while Freddie tried to make light chat, entertaining Jemima with stories from their revue days. She felt determined to help these two tired old men, odd but fundamentally kind and caring. Freddie rose from the table, having finished the featherlight souffle he had cooked for them, and wandered across to the piano, on which he started to play a rather jaunty tune.

'Our one real . . . I suppose what you'd call "hit", today. It's called "Hanging Around for You", sung actually by the Duchess — Eloise Claire as was. We thought we'd follow it up. We knew that Cocky, that is C. B. Cochrane, was looking for material for another review, and Cecil came up with this lovely tango. I added the lyrics, little knowing what a commotion they would cause.'

Freddie sang:

Oh, the Duchess danced.
The cream of all society was at the Duchess's ball.
A little Harlem ragtime band was playing in the hall.
They played a rhythm that was rather new
And they carried with 'em every dancing shoe,
For princes pranced and counts cavorted.
Barons bounced as well.
And then her Grace — oh, who would have thought it? —
Fell beneath the spell.

Whilst Freddie had been singing, Cecil seemed to pull himself together, slowly raised himself out of his chair, and crossed over to the piano. Together, the brothers sang the refrain:

Oh, the Duchess danced
When she heard that Tango.
Each time, she fanned her face.
Yes, the Duchess danced
At the syncopation.
Oh, what a sensation!
They all said, 'Attagirl, Your Grace.'

For a moment, Jemima saw the brothers as they must have appeared sixty years before, as young blades entertaining top society. She was transported back to another era.

'That did for us with Eloise Claire,' explained Freddie, shutting the piano lid. 'We weren't to know that this was the time that the Duke of Montfort had started taking an interest in her. She wasn't at all pleased. She thought we knew much more than in fact we did, and that we'd leak the story to the press. I'm afraid the Prideaux copybooks were a bit blotted there. We rather removed ourselves from the Castle Dorvan guest list.'

'Ah, so you have an old grudge against the Duchess?' exclaimed Jemima.

'Sixty years ago?' retorted Freddie. 'Surely you don't think . . .?'

'No, I'm sorry. It's just that we are clutching at straws. There's no evidence,' explained Jemima.

'Oh yes there is.' Cecil turned to Jemima and slowly brought something out of his pocket. 'Here you are. Something I found in one of Kenneth's jackets the day after he was killed.' He thrust a small, grubby, lined notebook into Jemima's hands. 'It's very private. I didn't want to show it to anyone. He writes about us in it, but at the end there are notes, and as you're so kindly trying to help me – you must have a look . . .' Cecil broke off and, picking up a bottle of whisky from the table, shambled out of the room. Freddie gazed sadly after him.

Jemima felt uncomfortable, an intruder in an immensely private moment of grief. As a very private person herself, she understood the bravery of Cecil's gesture. 'I don't think I should read this,' she said, as the crackly sound of a twenties' 78 came from Cecil's room. 'One of our records,' noted Freddie. 'Poor Cecil! He can't understand the world has changed. No, do look at his book. He *wanted* you to read it, otherwise he wouldn't have given it to you.'

Jemima opened the dog-eared notebook. The writing was truly appalling. She turned to the back pages, remembering what Cecil had said. 'Look,' she said to Freddie, unusually excited. 'Here's a mention of Eloise Claire:

' "Eloise Claire/Martha Cross – July to October 1920. Proof in Old Dairy in Box." Old Dairy?'

'Probably poor Kenneth's spelling. I expect it should read "Diary".'

'Yes, yes,' cried Jemima. 'He found an old diary which . . .' her mind raced, 'which implicated the Duchess in some illicit love affair, a scandal, something worthy of blackmail.'

Freddie caught Jemima's enthusiasm. 'And the diary's in a box.'

'Now that's the question.' The two subsided as the initial burst of enthusiasm had got them no further. They had searched the flat, and there was definitely no diary in any box that they could see.

'Shall we ask Cecil?' Freddie shook his head. 'No, best to let him rest and calm down now. I do, however, have an idea that might amuse you. Do you fancy a trip down Memory Lane?'

Memory Lane turned out to be St Martin's Lane, or rather one of those small alleyways in the heart of London's theatreland that lead off from there. Running east–west, connecting St Martin's Lane with Covent Garden, the pedestrian walkways were full of small overcrowded shops, ticket agencies, old-print galleries, and specialist bookshops. It was a perfect area in which to spend an afternoon browsing, and Jemima had to be dragged away from going through a box of second-hand books out on the pavement in front of one of her favourite shops. This time their destination was Tony Jerrold's shop 'Stage Whispers', an Aladdin's cave of theatrical memorabilia.

Tony himself was a character. Sitting behind his desk, he was engaged in camp bitchy chat on the telephone when Jemima and Freddie entered. They waved, and Tony continued with his conversation, patting his rather obvious toupé.

'I know my dear. Couldn't direct an old lady across the street. No, I'm not saying she's not talented,' bitched Tony into the mouthpiece of the telephone. 'I'm sure she's got a talent for something. Market gardening, maybe?'

What a delight of a shop, thought Jemima, as Tony prattled on. Each wall was covered from floor to ceiling by shelves holding memoirs, theatrical histories – anything which could be connected with the theatre. The tiny shop was filled with tables covered with boxes of old postcards, magazines and old theatre programmes. Jemima had entered a geriatric theatre world over the past few days that she found quite entrancing.

'Sorry love, I'm going to have to ring off to give the old body time to assimilate that. Have to tuck myself up in bed with a Valium sandwich to recover. Bysie-bye.' Tony put the phone down, took his feet off the desk, swivelled round in his chair, got up and, mincing, turned to Freddie. 'Sorry love – Vivienne, and you know what she's like when she's spilling the beans. And Miss Shore. How delightful to meet you. You don't happen to be "investigating" here by any chance?'

Jemima smiled. 'You wouldn't happen to have a bit of background on Eloise Claire would you?'

'On the Dancing Duchess? I must say, you're in luck.' Tony Jerrold dived under the counter and produced an old scrapbook which he passed across to Jemima and Freddie. 'Only came in last week. Some old buffer died, and his daughter brought it in thinking it might be worth a bob or two. At least she didn't throw it away as so many do – no interest in the past, no soul. He was a great fan of hers. Here, have a look.'

Together, Freddie and Jemima turned the dry, faded pages. There were programmes from old reviews, dried flowers, photos, menus – 'Dinners after the show at the Ivy, naturally,' explained Freddie. A small, oval, faded photograph of the Duchess fell out. Jemima bent over to pick it up from the floor, and couldn't help but exclaim at her beauty. 'She could drive sane men mad,' commented Freddie. Eloise's stage history was documented here like a biography except, Freddie observed there was one big gap.

'Nothing after "Joy Bells" at the Hippodrome . . .'

'Opened 25th March 1919,' Tony automatically chipped in.

'. . . until "Jumble Sale" at the Vaudeville,' Freddie responded.

'16th December 1920,' came back Tony.

'And "Joy Bells" didn't run eighteen months.'

'So what was she up to in between?' Jemima looked at the two old boys. 'That is what we have to find out.'

'Hang about loves, just a thought,' said Tony. 'I've a boxette here from Eulalie Vance's niece. She was a great chum of Eloise. You never know, you might find something there.' He jumped up onto his stepladder, and pulled down from one of the shelves a large old-fashioned chocolate box, tied up with an old red ribbon.

'How sad,' said Jemima as she pulled a faded satin heart from the box. 'That's half the attraction, my dear,' grinned Tony.

'I say, look at this.' Freddie was waving a picture postcard. 'A card from Eloise to Eulalie in "Just Fancy" at the Vaudeville.'

'Opened 26th March 1920,' intoned Tony.

'Just the right time,' said Jemima excitedly. 'Let's have

a look.' Freddie passed the card over to her, which Jemima read out loud.

' "Mother keeping pretty cheerful, but getting weaker every day." Well, that'd explain it – she was nursing a dying mother. Let's see.' She looked at the address; 'Well House, Sycamore Lane, Minchinhampton. That's Gloucestershire, isn't it? I suppose that's worth checking out.'

Jemima had already spent long past a normal lunch hour with the Prideaux brothers, and used Tony's phone to ring into Cherry for her messages. Cherry expressed boredom with the afternoon so Jemima despatched her off to Gloucestershire to check on the address from the postcard. 'Put it down to the abuse of expense-account story,' said Jemima. She knew that Cherry would enjoy a little bit of sleuthing away from the office, and that she wouldn't be averse to slapping some expenses on Megalith. Cherry would find the most expensive hotel in the length and breadth of the county to stay in and, no doubt, following her Paris experiences, would find plenty to criticise in the kitchen.

Jemima and Fedddie were feeling rather pleased with their progress, and were looking forward to telling Cecil their news. They had been in the flat only a few moments before they realised something was wrong. The sounds of a stuck gramophone record echoed round the flat. The refrain from their old song crackled out: 'Hanging around, hanging around, hanging around.' Jemima and Freddie looked at each other in horror. Freddie dashed across to Cecil's door, and as he opened it Jemima shrank back instinctively in horror. Silhouetted in the doorway was Cecil's body, hanging from the ceiling. 'Oh my God!' exclaimed Freddie, as he turned to Jemima, shutting the door. 'Cecil would be joking to the very end . . .'

In the days that followed, with the police and inquest, Jemima grew very close to Freddie, who had few friends to give him support. She was determined to get to the bottom of Kenneth Exton's death, but had got no further. Cherry's expedition to Gloucestershire had produced nothing except such a huge bill that Jemima doubted whether it would be passed by the accounts department. The address on the postcard had never existed.

Cecil's funeral was a bleak affair. The only other mourner, apart from Jemima and Freddie, was Tony Jerrold, and Jemima had her doubts about his motives when he asked Freddie and herself to sign the order of service. 'Like a programme,' he said, as she shook her head and remarked: 'You're incorrigible.'

'I know. That's part of my charm. And now, if you'll excuse me, I must do my parting credits number and vanish over the horizon. Byee.' And he scampered off down the path.

'Soul of tact,' murmured Jemima, but Tony had given Jemima a clue at long last.

'No, don't worry. He does care.' Freddie spoke out as he kicked the loose gravel on the graveyard path. 'I'm glad that Cecil's gone in a way,' he said, clenching and unclenching his fists. 'He's happier out of it. He always suffered, but since Kenneth's death he has suffered too much.' He stopped for a moment, and looked across the gravestones sticking up like irregular teeth through the half-mown grass. 'I think we'd *both* be better out of it. We belong to a world that no longer exists. Went long ago.' He finally gave vent to his pain and anger. 'I want her to suffer too, you know. She did kill him, even if she didn't know it. She murdered him. Sorry —' he shuffled nervously, 'not the usual Freddie Prideaux.' Jemima squeezed his arm affectionately: the dear old soul had taken a lot of knocks, and he was the perfect gentleman, letting his sadness show through only for a moment. 'Any ideas Jem? I think we've come to a dead end. There's no box, no diary, that I can find.'

Jemima looked at Freddie, her thoughts suddenly clarifying. 'Yes, I have. And it's Tony Jerrold who triggered them. I've remembered someone who is as TV-struck as Tony is stage-struck, and he might be able to help us.'

Jemima returned to her swish office at Megalithic House. In contrast to her romantic pine-furnished flat, her office glistened with high-tech efficiency: matt-black cabinets and shelves, and two very executive desks for herself and Cherry. She poured herself some coffee from the filter machine that kept a permanent supply on tap for her. One of Jemima's pet hates was instant coffee, and Cherry's job would be on the line the day she forgot to put the coffee machine on.

Sipping her coffee from a large white and pink cup, Jemima phoned the Duchess of Montfort's residence.

Tupper seemed to jump at Jemima's request for an interview on the spurious grounds that she was going to do a programme about domestic service and wanted to discuss the art of buttling with him. Jemima suggested he came to her office to avoid any risk of embarrassing his employer.

However, the interview proved more difficult than she anticipated. He was not the buffoon he initially appeared. He politely answered all Jemima's questions about buttling, but as soon as she wanted to know more direct information about the Duchess, he turned wary.

'Without being rude, Miss Shore, it is perfectly clear to me that you are more concerned with the most unfortunate incident of Exton's death than with any background to service,' Tupper finally announced after Jemima had asked him where he had been the night of the killing.

'I was walking Mason, Miss Shore. The Duchess said he had got over-excited.'

'So Kenneth Exton came and had been shot whilst you were out of the house. Had the Duchess called the police?'

'No. I did that Miss Shore. The Duchess was clearing up the mess.'

Jemima's questions as to what a pair of Purdys — sporting guns — were doing in a town house met with equally short shrift although with a convincing answer. 'After the Duke died, the Duchess decided to move permanently to London. I asked permission to keep the guns in town so that I could clean and grease them regularly.

'I explained all this and more to the police, Miss Shore. I do not think your prying will uncover any dirt. Her Grace has already been through the courts once, and was exonerated. I don't know what you think your investigations are going to find. We have nothing to hide.'

With that, Tupper walked out of Jemima's office. She sat back to sort out what he had told her. At the end of it all, there was only one new piece of information, and that was that the Duke's wartime gun had been reported stolen some months previously, and that it was a Luger. 'A Luger.' That make of the gun was familiar, Jemima thought. The Duchess had said that her intruder, Kenneth Exton, had pulled a Luger on her. Maybe he hadn't. Maybe it had been planted.

Jemima wandered up and down her office. Thank goodness the interview had taken place in the privacy of her office, and with Cherry out of the way. Tupper had made her feel very foolish, but her suspicions were still being confirmed. The Exton case was not all it seemed, but she had still got no further in her attempt to vindicate Cecil's belief in Kenneth's innocence. She broadened her review: *nothing* seemed to be going her way. Leo Squire was continually pestering her to such an extent that she would *have* to agree to have dinner with him, even if it was so as to be extremely un-Jemima-like, and be very rude. She decided on clearing up the office. This was a routine which she always used to calm her mind and collect her thoughts. She threw all the old newspapers into the wastepaper basket, piled all the long-overdue library books on a side desk, and was sorting through a pile of long and gushy fan letters that she would have to reply to individually, when she spotted the map of Gloucestershire that Cherry had used on her travels. She spread it out on the glass-and-chrome coffee table in the middle of the office, and searched for Minchinhampton. She'd never been too sure where it was – and there it was. She couldn't believe it. The clue they had been looking for was staring her in the face.

At this moment, Cherry walked back into the office. Jemima stared at her frostily. She sometimes despaired. 'Did you look at the map at all when you went up to Gloucestershire,' she asked, rather tartly. Cherry wandered over to the table and shook her head looking expectantly, 'Er, no. Why? Should I have done?'

'We're idiots – no, I'm an idiot, I'm an idiot,' intoned Jemima. 'Here, have a look at the map.' Cherry leant over the coffee table, and there it was, staring her in the face – the name 'Box'. Box was a village near Minchinhampton. Cherry looked at the floor, and had the grace to blush. There was nothing she could say. Jemima looked at her and they both giggled. It was so obvious – too obvious, and they had both missed it.

'Come on,' said Jemima as she leapt up and strode across the room. 'We're going back to the country.'

Jemima was moved to exalt the virtues of the motorway system as they sped down the M4, until Cherry pointed out this was deeply ironic, because Jemima had made several programmes siding with the motorway protesters, exposing the iniquity of weekend cottages which were made a feasible proposition only by the building of motorways, and opposing the increase in size of lorries. It all made Cherry feel marginally better, because she had failed to come up with a satisfactory answer – even for herself – as to why she hadn't spotted the most elementary of clues.

They came off the motorway and slowly drove through Cotswold lanes, bounded by dry-stone walls, to Box. Entering the village from the top, Jemima drove right through it, until they came to a house on the outskirts, surrounded by a large well-ordered garden, and with a large hoarding attached to the stone wall. Kenneth's spelling had been correct all along. The sign read: OLD DAIRY PRIVATE HOTEL.

Using the expert Jemima Shore mixture of charm and persistence, Jemima persuaded the Matron to let her see the old lady who had been visited by Kenneth Exton several months previously. 'She'll talk nonsense,' said the Matron. 'I really don't know what you'll get out of her.'

The old lady's name was Minnie, and she was sitting in a conservatory day room, overlooking the grounds. To Jemima, she seemed sharper than the Matron. She looked testily at Jemima.

'So you've come about the baby too?' she said.

'Yes?' asked Jemima, trying not to show her excitement.

'A boy. Named Edgar. Born 16th September 1920.' Jemima and Cherry exchanged significant looks. 'It was an easy birth; she was so supple. You could tell she was a dancer.'

Jemima leant forward. 'What happened to the baby?'

'Fostered at a week old. Fostered in the village.' The old lady started to slump forward as if to doze off. She then suddenly started up and pulled Jemima down close to her. 'They called him Kenneth.' At this point, Jemima looked up to see Tupper enter the day room. They looked each other in the face.

'I have the information I need now, Tupper,' said Jemima. 'I think you're too late for whatever you had plans to do.' Jemima felt a small sensation of pleasure at having pipped him to the post – a man who managed to be both obsequious and rude in just about equal amounts.

Jemima and Cherry drove back to London in the greatest excitement. Before she said anything to Freddie, Jemima sent Cherry down to St Catherines House to trace the child's birth certificate, and then if that all fitted to meet at Freddie's flat.

'There's absolutely no doubt about it,' Jemima said to Freddie. 'It's all here on the birth certificate. Mother – Martha Cross. Father – unknown. Child named Edgar. Abandoned so she could pursue her own ambitions.'

'It seems a shame that one mistake meant so much in those days,' said the thoroughly modern Cherry.

'Oh, it did, my dear. It could ruin a girl. It most certainly would have prevented her marrying the Duke if that sort of thing was known about.' Freddie looked at the two women. 'What now? The police? It seems clear to me that her son Kenneth – never able to do a decent, straightforward thing – was trying to blackmail her. He didn't have time or the inclination to tell her who he really was, and she shot him!'

'We've got no firm evidence,' stated Jemima. 'I think it is time I paid the Duchess another visit.'

Jemima felt quite apprehensive as she stood outside the Duchess's home once more. She had left Cherry in the car with strict instructions to call the police if she wasn't out within the hour. Tupper opened the front door and looked at Jemima without a flicker of surprise.

'I think Mason may need another walk,' Jemima said acidly as she was let in, noting the supine dog at the bottom of the stairs. It was a long climb up the stairs to the Duchess's drawing room — and what if her deductions were wrong? No, they couldn't be. Her conclusions were the correct ones.

The Duchess was standing with her back to the room, looking into the fire, as Jemima entered. She turned to face Jemima, her lips pursed and eyes blazing with rage.

'And is your aim also blackmail, Miss Shore?' she demanded. Jemima kept on walking and extended her hand to the Duchess. Even in moments of high tension such as this, her good manners never left her. 'No. My aim is justice,' she said, staring at the Duchess, who indicated that she should sit down. There was no champagne, no small talk, this time.

'How very quaint, how very old-fashioned. I made a mistake at sixteen, and I chose to keep it a secret. Is that such a crime? Does that merit the talk of justice?'

'I wasn't talking about that, Duchess. I was talking about the killing of Kenneth Exton.' Jemima continued, 'Yes, Kenneth Exton, the blackmailer. He came here, and you shot him not in self-defence, but in cold blood, and planted the Luger on him.'

The Duchess laughed at Jemima, tapping her feet on one of the firedogs. 'Even if that were true, Miss Shore, it is irrelevant. He was a common little blackmailer trying to blacken my name. He deserved to die just as much as if he had drawn a gun on me.'

Jemima could not believe she was listening to such determined selfishness. Here was a woman with no remorse. She leant forward. 'He didn't tell you then,

Duchess, how he found out about the child. Do you wonder how he knew about the baby?'

The Duchess walked across from the fire and sat opposite Jemima in one of her elegant, straight-backed chairs. 'No. He just suggested we met to discuss the price of his silence.'

'In the same way that Tupper was going to discuss Minnie's silence?' responded Jemima.

The Duchess drew herself up and snapped at Jemima. 'Wrong, Miss Shore. If you must know, Tupper was bound on a similar mission to your own. I told you I wanted to leave my wealth to someone. I wanted to leave it to my son.'

Jemima looked at her unbelievingly. Could it be possible that the Duchess really did not know who Kenneth Exton was? The Duchess continued, 'By all means pursue your pursuit of justice, Miss Shore, but you have no evidence, and he was hardly worthy of your interest and concern. He was hardly a hero, my dear. A very third-rate little man.'

Jemima rose to go. There was nothing more to do. She walked across the room, and before she left she asked the direct question: 'Did Kenneth Exton tell you the details of what he knew?'

The Duchess shook her head.

'That was a pity, Duchess,' Jemima continued, 'because what Kenneth Exton had come to tell you was that he was born on 16th September 1920 in Minchinhampton. Kenneth Exton, Duchess, was your son . . .'

Jemima just glanced at the expression on the Duchess's face before she left the room. Justice had been done. It was not an experience she would care to repeat. In fact, a Prideaux Heartfonder was probably called for. As she climbed into the driving seat of her Mercedes, she told Cherry to book a table at the Ivy. She would be having dinner after the show – and it wouldn't be with Leo Squire.

# A Greek Bearing Gifts

They came in quick succession: first a Greek bearing a lost cat, then a policeman bearing bad news.

Neither of them got a warm welcome. During an especially wintry week, Jemima Shore's flat had been deprived of heat, and promises that all would soon be put right were on the same level of credibility as the Post Office's repeated assurances that first-class letters nearly always arrived first post the next day. Jemima had spent an hour in the morning trying to keep warm by playing squash, resulting in near-collapse on a bench in the gymnasium. An equally exhausted young man with a dark, damp complexion had spoken briefly to her but without any obvious interest. A preliminary interview for one of her investigative programmes had gone off the rails and she was having to reshuffle the whole basic pattern.

On top of all this, her Mercedes had developed a migraine, and the substitute Volkswagen offered on loan by the garage was enough to provide Jemima herself with the makings of a similarly distressing migraine.

And where on earth was Midnight, her cat? She wouldn't have put it past him to have deserted and gone in search of warmer premises – not that *she* would have minded finding just such premises right now. Huddled in her coat beside a dismal little blower-heater, she tried to concentrate on her notes; but every few minutes she had to get up and turn back a rug on the couch, or go into the kitchen yet again in search of the missing Midnight.

There was a ring at the doorbell. Irritated by this further interruption, she went to answer, cautiously keeping the door on its chain.

Through the opening, she was faced by a man in chauffeur's uniform. He had dark olive eyes and what could only be described as a classic Grecian nose.

'May I speak with Mr Shore?'

'Hardly. I'm *Miss* Shore.'

'You will please receive my master? It is proper that I ask. He cannot speak to someone to whom he has not been presented.'

Jemima stared, baffled. 'When does he want to be presented — and why?'

'Now,' said a voice from beyond the chauffeur. 'Because he has something for you.'

Another face was framed in the gap. It was younger and a great deal more compelling, though equally dark. Jemima warily appraised the newcomer. His clothes were expensive — that dark overcoat was austerely cut but not, she was sure, austerely priced — and there was the glint of a wide gold watch-strap on his wrist. The sleeve had been drawn back from that wrist as his fingers gripped the edge of a cardboard box labelled 'Dom Perignon'. All at once, she remembered his face.

Trusting her own snap judgment, she slipped the chain and held the door open. The young man walked in; the chauffeur stayed outside.

'Won't you take your coat off?' said Jemima.

Her visitor shivered. 'You like it so cold?'

'I'm tough. And surprised to see you again so soon.' The features were those she had fleetingly taken in, without interest, at the gymnasium that morning. She felt a prickle of doubt at such an odd coincidence. 'And I must say straight away, Mr . . .?'

'Karydas. Nicky Karydas.'

'Jemima Shore. Who must say that she can't accept wine, least of all champagne, which she's far too cold to drink. And least of all from a strange man.'

'Of course you can't,' he said smoothly. 'Actually, I assumed J. Shore was also a man. I have something which belongs to you.'

He opened the box. Midnight's dark head came out, and Midnight said something obscene as Nicky Karydas crooked a finger under his collar. 'You see, here it is – J. Shore. He spent some time sitting on the bonnet of my motor-car.'

'Because it was nice and warm.' Jemima reached out to stroke Midnight, though he didn't deserve it. 'Now, can I offer you a drink? Not champagne, I'm afraid, but quite a decent Meursault.'

Midnight followed her into the kitchen, rubbing against her legs, and followed her back out again as she carried a bottle and two glasses to the coffee table. He tried to climb on the sofa between her and Nicky Karydas as they sat down, but Jemima removed him – gently enough, but all the same, he trotted off to the far side of the room and he ostentatiously washed himself as if to destroy all traces of her touch.

As Jemima raised her glass, there was a murmur of voices on the landing outside. The chauffeur raised his. Another man spoke in a lower tone, firm and authoritative. Then the doorbell rang again.

'You have another cat?' said Nicky.

This time the face in the doorway was one she was

usually glad to see. Today it looked unusually grave. She let her old friend in and introduced him to Nicky.

'Police?' Nicky feigned alarm. 'Orestes is badly parked?'

'We leave that to the traffic wardens, sir,' said Detective Chief Inspector Portsmouth.

Something in his manner had an immediate effect on the young Greek. He was on his feet, turning towards the door, saying 'Thanks for your hospitality' and bowing to kiss Jemima's hand. One of Portsmouth's eyebrows jerked disapprovingly into the angle of an automatic crossing barrier with doubts about an oncoming train.

When they were alone together, Jemima said: 'Something wrong, Pompey?'

'They'd have sent a sergeant, or you might have had to wait until you saw it in the papers, but it came to my attention, so I thought I'd drop in personally.'

'What came to your attention?'

Pompey, generally a direct and forceful man, seemed reluctant to get the words out. 'There have been calls from the Stutworth police. You know, Stutworth in –'

'Oh, no. Something about . . . about the General?'

'Major-General Ballister. I know he was a friend of yours.'

A friend? She had known him all her life. And he had been as right as ninepence when she saw him only a week ago. Wanting her to get him a book, fussing amiably about it and fussing about his paraffin lamp. There was no electricity in his cottage, and he swore he didn't want it: much more restful light from his lamp, he insisted.

'He's dead?' When Pompey nodded, she pleaded: 'It was peaceful?'

'No, Jemima. I'm afraid it wasn't. He burned to death.

A lamp exploded. Stutworth have worked out that petrol got into the paraffin. When he lit it —'

'Petrol?'

'Old people get careless.'

'Not Major-Generals. Least of all that one.'

She was stunned. Of course old friends had to die sometime; of course Major-General Ballister had had a good innings; but, after surviving so many dangers during his life on active service, to be burned to death in his own home . . .

There was no family to mourn him. Just herself. He had always treated Jemima not just as a kid, but as one of his own kids; and still, right to the end, thought of her that way. When she had been at school, every Christmas he had sent a card with a pound note in it. This last Christmas there had been the card and the pound note just the same as ever.

'I'll go down tomorrow,' she said as she opened the door to let Pompey out. 'There's nobody else to . . . tidy up.' She tried to keep her voice steady. 'Thanks for coming round. It was sweet of you.'

Tears came helplessly into her eyes as he walked away. Before she could close the door again, Nicky Karydas was there, pushing in and putting his arms round her. 'I had to be sure you were all right. I mean, police! You need rescuing?'

'A bit of bad news. An old friend. My father's commanding officer . . . I . . .'

'Do you good to cry.' He drew her even closer and let her bury her head in his shoulder.

She tugged away. 'I must ring the station, find out an early train. I can't drive that horrible car all the way.'

'You will use my car. Orestes will drive you. I insist. It will please me to please you.'

She was too numbed to argue. It was a relief to let

someone else make the decisions for her. A relief, next day, to sit in the Rolls and let her thoughts settle down. By the time they reached the cottage down its country lane she had talked herself into believing that she could do such routine things as had to be done impersonally and efficiently, salvaging perhaps some little thing of sentimental value to herself and working out what the rest would fetch towards funeral and other expenses. But the sight of the cottage came as a shock.

One of the windows had been blown out, another was starred with cracks, and the lintels and door-jambs were smeared by greasy smoke stains. What was left of the General's armchair lay in a twisted heap between the cottage and the garden shed, reminding her too achingly, too vividly, of him.

Orestes sat impassively in the car as she walked round the damaged building and into the shed with its litter of tools, jam jars, and scraps of wood. The General had been an inveterate hoarder. From one box she picked out a handful of what looked like school exercise-books. As she was about to examine them, she heard a faint, eerie, faraway call.

'Je – mi – ma . . .'

She went out and gazed over the ragged hedge into the shadows of the plantation and the undergrowth beyond.

'Je – mi – ma . . .'

It was like the plaintive cry of some ghost wanting to communicate with her. But the footsteps clumping through the tangle of branches and dead leaves were real enough; and so, to her dismay, were the couple who emerged and glared at her.

Ten-year-old Jemima Jarvis made a face at her. The child's father clutched his shotgun and growled: 'And what are you supposed to be doing here? This is my property. You're trespassing on my property.'

'You're not slow to claim it.'

'The tenancy's expired. You can't take anything.'

'Now the cottage is empty,' the girl gloated, 'my granny's going to live in it.'

There was really nothing to say. Jemima had never had anything much to say to the Jarvis family, and could only wonder how the General had endured them as neighbours for so long. He had even stood as godfather to this spiteful little brat, and maybe that was why she had come to be called Jemima – for all the good that appeared to have done anyone.

Jarvis stood with his gun under his arm waiting for her to move away. There was no word of regret, no commiseration.

Jemima walked back to the lane, refusing to hurry. Orestes was out of the car before she reached it, holding the door open.

The younger Jemima came skipping after her. 'I told the policeman about *you*. How you came to see him.' She edged up alongside the car. 'I killed a rabbit yesterday. I'm going to make myself some gloves.' She brandished a small knife; and, as the Rolls pulled gently away up the lane, suddenly turned it so that a long scratch was gouged into the paintwork.

Jemima sat back and closed her eyes. An accident, she said silently to herself over and over again, of course it was an accident. Even creatures like the Jarvises would hardly commit murder just to regain possession of the cottage.

There had been no sign of the paraffin or petrol in the shed: no cans, no filler, or anything else. Presumably the police had taken them away.

It had to be an accident.

She went straight to Megalith Television, to be greeted by a flurry of conflicting messages and some sly asides.

'We thought you'd left us and gone to work for the BBC,' was Guthrie's opening gambit. (Guthrie Carlyle directs Jemima's show.)

'You have a meeting with Cy and the Chairman of the Board tomorrow at two-thirty,' said Cherry. (Cy Fredericks is Managing Director and Programme Controller of Megalith.) 'Oh, and there's a lady waiting to see you. And a man rang to ask if you'd got it.'

'Got it?'

From beneath the desk Cherry extracted a long be-ribboned box and laid it before Jemima. She and Guthrie were obviously longing to know what was in it.

They groaned as she opened it to reveal a foam of white roses.

'Doesn't it make you sick!' said Guthrie.

Cherry bent enviously over the box. 'At this time of year!'

Jemima removed the card from its silk ribbon. At the top it said: 'Beauty for the most beautiful.' Then, lower down: 'I beg you to dine with me tonight. Just the two of us. Or you may bring the cat as chaperon. Yours, as you already know – Nicky Karydas.'

'Find a vase,' she said. 'And you'd better wheel in the visitor before she starts growing cobwebs.'

Cherry ushered in an elderly middle-aged woman with a diffident smile but an oddly determined jut to her chin. Guthrie mumbled an excuse and slipped out, leaving the two women together.

'My name's Westrop,' said the visitor directly. 'Dorothy Westrop. I've come about Major-General Ballister.'

'He's dead.'

'I know. A friend rang. It was in their local paper this morning.'

'You knew him?'

'Ages ago. My husband was in his lot. Captain Westrop – Jerry Westrop, your father's adjutant.'

Jemima sought to conjure up some echo from her memory, but the name meant nothing. She had been very young at the time, and so many grown-up people and so many names had come and gone.

Mrs Westrop said: 'Your father . . .' She hesitated.

'Yes?'

'Colonel Shore also died in an accident.'

'A long time ago,' Jemima nodded, 'in Hong Kong.'

'My husband died in France – in an accident. And now General Ballister, here in England. It looks like the whole chain of command, doesn't it?'

There was indeed an unhappy irony in it: the General, the Colonel, the Captain – but not, thought Jemima, in that order.

'And all accidents.' Mrs Westrop's voice hardened and all at once she was punching the words home. 'Over the years they're bound to go, one after the other, all right. But *all* accidents? Three bright, highly trained officers? What would you say the odds were, Miss Shore . . . *Investigator*? Mm?'

Jemima was still turning it over in her mind as she dressed for her dinner date that evening. It was all silly, of course: a wild speculation; but it kept nagging at her. Three of them, so closely connected, in such circumstances . . .

Be sensible about it, she told herself. The three deaths had occurred over a space of some twenty-five years.

Only it had not been quite like that. Her father had died a long time ago, yes; but Captain Westrop not so long ago, and the General just now. 'Accidental death' would be the verdict on the General. And why not? Jemima studied her hair in the glass, and prodded at an awkward strand above her left ear. She wished she had visited the old man more often. Would that have shaken events into a different shape, so that he would have lived? She thought of those nasty, niggling Jarvises – and realised she was probably looking for someone else to blame so that she did not have to blame herself.

Further fretting and speculation were ended by the arrival of Orestes with the Rolls. She was whisked luxuriously away to the house in Breck Place, where Nicky Karydas was waiting for her. On the doorstep, as Orestes stood aside watching her expressionlessly, she took a deep breath. For the rest of this evening it would be the present she'd have to cope with, not the past.

The meal was all she could have desired. The unobtrusive background music was as dreamy and quietly suggestive as she might have expected. The drawing room, where Orestes served coffee and then withdrew, was almost too sumptuous and relaxing.

It was a room in which one might well have seen beautifully bound books. Instead, an old paperback with yellowing pages lay open, face down on the arm of a chair. Curiously Jemima picked it up: other people's reading matter was always provocative. She had hardly expected to find that Nicky had been reading Bernard Shaw's *Caesar and Cleopatra*; and she wondered why he had chosen to mark one passage:

Horror unspeakable! The fire has spread from your ships. The first of the seven wonders of the world perishes. The library of Alexandria is in flames. Will Caesar go down to posterity as a barbarian soldier too ignorant to know the value of books? Without books, death will lay you beside your meanest soldier.

Questioned by Nicky's half-amused, half-searching gaze, Jemima said: 'Shaw – I'm not keen.'

'Because he doesn't put women on pedestals?'

'Because he spells his name wrongly.'

He looked puzzled, then laughed. 'Ah, I see. Only your way of spelling it is correct?'

'Of course.'

Nicky took the paperback from her and, before she could guess at his intention, threw it on to the fire. 'Nothing must displease you.'

'Your gesture displeases me,' she said, disturbed.

He said: 'I should like to know why you're not married.'

Jemima gasped. 'You come on a bit strong.'

'If I do, it's because my feelings are strong.'

He seemed to be hamming it a bit, spreading his arms, yearning at her with just a bit too much ardour. What did he want: a few hours' pleasure, fast and lustful and furious, and then a farewell wave? Jemima found it difficult to ask herself the same question. He had a burning intensity that frightened her yet drew her on. She was not at all sure that she would be able to continue asking rational, hard-headed questions if he went on looking at her like this.

'You don't know me,' she said weakly.

'I know you very well.' At last he lowered his eyes, and smiled an almost humble smile – genuine, or still part of that strange act of his? 'Jemima, I've deceived you. Only the once, and I promise never to do it again. You surely haven't forgotten you're public property in thousands of homes?' He nodded at a television screen across the room. 'I was in London a while ago, bored. So I watch television. A woman was on, a programme about lonely childhoods.'

Jemima remembered it: a one-off, not at all her usual sort of thing, talking about herself.

'I managed not to fall in love with her,' said Nicky, 'for about a minute or two.'

'Did you kidnap my cat as a way of meeting me?'

'I see I must tread very carefully.'

'Lonely childhoods,' she echoed. 'Why were you so interested?'

'My aunt brought me up. My father died before I was born. My mother when I was ten.'

'Both of mine died in a car crash in Hong Kong.'

He was staring eagerly at her again, demanding something from her, almost terrifying in his concentration. 'You see how well suited we are? In due course I shall ask you to marry me.'

It was too much; too swift; too absurd. Jemima waved a dismissive hand, only to find that he had trapped it and was coaxing her to her feet and out into the middle of the room, dancing to the slow tempo of the muted music. She rested her cheek on his fingers as they crept up on to her shoulder. Once again the sleeve had fallen back from his wrist, and escaping from the edge of his watchstrap was a wrinkle of skin with what looked like a tattoo on it. As she lowered and turned her head to make out the figures better, she sensed that he was taking this as an encouragement. She pulled away, and was thankful that the tune had stopped.

In the interval before the next number on the tape she said: 'It's getting late. I must go.'

'Please, I do not want you to leave. Not so soon.'

'I'm still a working girl, with a lot of work first thing tomorrow.'

He shrugged, more readily than she had anticipated. 'So. I get your coat, and I drive you home.'

While he was out of the room she looked, uneasy again, at the flickering shreds of transparent blackness which were all that remained of the Shaw paperback. His impulses, she was beginning to appreciate, were swift and unpredictable. Her eyes roamed the mantelpiece above the fire, and reached a cluster of envelopes tucked behind a heavy candlestick. She was not prying . . . not really . . . just letting her attention wander. It wandered as far as the address on the top envelope; and she nudged that to one side and saw the addresses on the next couple. They were apparently all waiting here for a Miss Mary Glendenning at 28 Breck Place.

Behind her, Nicky said: 'She used to live here. I still get her mail, but I've no idea where to send it.'

He held out her coat and slid it expertly over her shoulders.

'Goodnight, Mr Karydas.'

'Mister . . .?'

'Goodnight, Nicky. And thank you for dinner. And for the glorious warmth.'

'It feels ungallant, letting you go so early.'

Gallantry, she thought when she reached home, was such an old-fashioned word. And really very pleasant. She was surprised that he had so readily agreed to her leaving his house; and could not decide whether to be mildly piqued or relieved.

Lying wide awake in bed, she tried to sort out her emotions as coolly as she would have sorted out the different aspects of a tricky television programme. Out of the confusion came, as it so often did, a striking fact. Nicky, before even approaching her, had acquired a lot of knowledge about her. He had – she was sure of this – kidnapped her cat in order to effect an introduction. Yet she knew nothing about him. Captivated by his smile and insidious manner, she had carried things off gracefully so far, but without much real insight. Who was Nicky Karydas, when you got down to it?

Who, for that matter, was Miss Mary Glendenning?

And a blurred image swam before her eyes – an image

of numbers, tattooed on Nicky's wrist. What could the 1–7–9–5–5 signify?

In the morning she gave Cherry a number of strange assignments, and shamelessly pretended that they had something to do with 'quite an idea I've got floating around in my mind'. Then she set off on a return trip to Stutworth, this time under her own steam.

The exercise-books were still stacked higgledy-piggledy, as she had seen them on that last visit. She was turning them over when, once again, there came an interruption.

Young Jemima said: 'I'll tell daddy. You've got no right to be here.' She was carrying an old but still effective-looking bayonet which must have come from the General's private hoard. 'What are you stealing?' she asked cunningly. 'I won't tell, if you ... if you bring me a compass. I want a compass.'

'Have you been in here before?' Jemima challenged.

'A million times.' The child was methodically cutting slivers from the workbench with the bayonet. 'I used to help him fill the lamps.'

Jemima stayed very still. 'Were the two cans alike, the paraffin and petrol?'

'Not a bit. Anyway, the petrol was empty. I used it for a bonfire.' The pale, unchildish eyes mocked the older Jemima. 'You'd like to ask me if I know who did it, wouldn't you? Who mixed it?'

'All right. Who mixed it – who put the petrol in?'

'I want a compass. A real one, a good one. Next time, bring me a compass.'

Before Jemima could stop her, the girl was at the door, fingering the blade and grinning.

'I wonder,' said Jemima Shore, 'what you'll be when you grow up.'

'Oh, I know that.' The blade turned in the chill sunlight. 'A brain surgeon.'

At least, thought Jemima as she drove herself bumpily back in the spluttering, grinding car, there had not been Mr Jarvis with his gun this time. This time she had brought the exercise-books away with her.

She was fingering through them in the production office while Cherry made phone calls and clucked in exasperation in the next room. Guthrie pored over the figures Jemima had scribbled out for him.

'A tattoo?' he said. 'On his wrist? We're going to do a programme about concentration camps?'

'He's too young for that. It could be a date.'

'Or the combination of a safe. These rich fiddlers, they've all got a Swiss bank account.'

'Who says he's on the fiddle?'

Before Guthrie could think up some snide remark, Cherry came in, riffling through her notebook with a satisfied air.

'Nicky Karydas,' she said dramatically. 'He exists all right.'

'I'm aware of that,' said Jemima.

'Family firm. Shipping magnates only more so. See a ship, buy it. Or build the odd dozen to fill in the time. Nicky on the board of directors, nominally. Only doesn't seem to play any active part in administration.'

'Layabout,' grunted Guthrie. 'Nothing better to do than –'

'Thank you,' said Jemima.

Cherry flipped over a page. 'Miss Mary Glendenning. Daughter of Lord Glendenning, life peer, and Lady Isobel, both deceased. Lives at 28 Breck Place and is *loaded*.'

'Still 28 Breck Place?'

'I checked,' said Cherry in an injured tone. 'That's her

pad. But every year, straight after Christmas she's off to her villa in Amalfi. Stays there till Easter. Every year, regular as clockwork, never misses.'

'And lets her London base to a rich Greek,' Guthrie mused.

Jemima felt a stir of doubt. With that sort of money, would a woman of that kind let her house?

She said: 'Any idea of the phone number in Amalfi?'

Cherry sagged. 'Italian directory inquiries? Okay, I'll be back in a week.'

Jemima returned to the exercise-books, smelling of damp and something indefinable which might have been a cocktail of paraffin, weed-killer, and rust. The neat but widely spaced handwriting gave her another pang, remembering Major-General Ballister's signature on a Christmas card and the expansive address on an envelope. Here were jottings covering several decades, not so much a diary as a spasmodic scribble of recollections back to when he had been a subaltern.

'Who'd want a date tattooed?' Guthrie was thinking out loud. 'Not an American date, anyway: that'd make it January the 79th. But do it our way, and you get 17–9–55. Seventeenth of September. Just a minute – wasn't that the anniversary of the Battle of Britain? I remember that from one of our programmes. But 1955 . . .'

Jemima stopped, jolted by the date on a curling page.

There it was, the seventeenth of September 1955. ' A day and night to be remembered and regretted,' she read. 'Colonel Shore was completely in the right, and his men, including Captain Westrop, right to obey him. But wisdom of the action in that atmosphere was far from certain. Results horrible. Tragic.'

Jemima reached for the telephone. One among the many advantages of working for Megalith Television was ready access to the most comprehensively indexed files of newspapers. Informed that a thorough search would take two hours, she decided to go out and follow up another lead. Or would it be a dead end?

Somehow she knew — and was far from cheered by knowing — that the two strands would come together and make sense in a way she might not enjoy.

She was even less cheered as she passed the little art gallery on her way to Sokrates' bookshop. A Dufy in the window had for some weeks cast its very special sunny glow down the cramped alley, and Jemima had felt nourished by it each time she went by. Now it was gone: sold, she supposed, to someone with similar tastes to her own but a lot more money.

The bookshop cast no kind of glow. Dust lay on the ancient tomes in its window, and dust added its patina to the shelves and stacks and bundles of books within. Mr Sokrates himself was an integral part of the décor, moving slowly and contentedly through the chaos as if not caring to risk any faster movement in case he disappeared in an enveloping, choking cloud.

Jemima wasted no words. 'Mr Sokrates, you're the only Greek I've known a long time. Do you know anything about a man called Karydas?'

'A Karydas wrote to me once. Nicholas Karydas. Asked me to bid at an auction for a George Bernard Shaw notebook.' He shrugged, and patted dust from his hands. 'I didn't get it.'

'You actually know him?'

'I don't know anyone. Only the addresses where I send books. I remember his address in France, it was so pretty. La Maison aux Rossignols at Marie-la-Petite. His mother,' he added, 'was the important one.'

'Mother?'

'Irene Karydas. Wrote many books. About her

country, about women. And some novels. None of them translated, so you wouldn't know her.'

'She's dead?'

'And all that money went to her son.'

'You wouldn't have any details about him – personally?'

'No more questions until you buy a book.' Sokrates paused a moment, then relented. 'He's not a playboy, or he would be in the newspapers. And he does not spend his money on good books. Not in here.' Craftily he added: 'I do have a book by his mother. In Greek. But it has her picture on it. Only three pounds.'

Jemima snorted, but took three notes from her bag. They vanished straight into his waistcoat pocket as he shuffled back into the recesses of the shop. The doorbell tinkled as someone else came in and edged along the shelves. Sokrates called something vague to the newcomer and returned, holding out a plump foreign paperback with roughly trimmed edges.

On the back was a studio photograph of a beautiful woman in her thirties. Jemima studied it, and thought ruefully how obvious it was where Nicky got his looks from. What a pity that, reading no Greek, she could not discover whether Irene Karydas's literary style was equally beautiful.

Turning towards the door, she saw the man who had come in a couple of minutes ago.

Orestes smiled awkwardly.

'Are you following me?' Jemima demanded.

'I go to Greek shops, Greek restaurants, on my day off. It makes foreign places less foreign.'

It sounded unconvincing. But why should Nicky want to have her followed? Jemima added to her other doubts the possibility that he was a dangerously jealous type. That was something she could do without, flattering as it might be.

She moved past Orestes.

Tensely he said: 'Miss Shore, I have wanted to speak to you. About my master. I think you are getting . . . fond of him?'

'Am I?' said Jemima coldly.

'And you must be . . . please, I think you should know that . . .'

His voice trailed away. He was staring at the book she was holding, with the photograph tilted in his direction.

'Know what?' asked Jemima.

'Nothing. I exceed my position. Forgive me.'

He almost ran from the shop.

Thoughtfully she made her way back to the flat. She ought to have gone back to the office, but they wouldn't have dug out those newspapers yet, and right now she was more and more obsessed by that question, and less and less interested in programme planning. She would have a quick snack at home and then give them a ring.

Propped against the skirting-board on her landing was a wide but slim brown-paper parcel. Even without stooping to pick it up she could read the bold lettering on the paper. It was addressed to Mrs Jemima Karydas.

'I know you're there,' she said loudly, far from pleased.

Nicky peeped round the corner of the landing and came towards her, opening his arms wide in an expansive gesture. She turned away to open the door, carried the parcel in, and stuffed the paperback out of sight behind a cushion. Then, accusingly, she tapped the writing on the brown paper.

'I thought you might start getting used to the name,' he said endearingly.

'You take a lot for granted.'

Nicky nodded at the package. 'Please open it.'

'Whatever it is, you can take it away again.'

'You think it's too soon? You do not like me today. You are in bad humour.'

'I don't like being followed.'

'Followed?' He looked genuinely puzzled. 'Who has followed you? Unless you mean *I'm* following you. But . . . someone else? Please tell me.'

Rather than pursue the matter, Jemima opened the parcel. Within lay that delectable Dufy painting.

Nicky said: 'I've seen you looking at it.'

'So you do follow me.'

'Lovers are great followers. And now, will you marry me?'

She dodged that one and said simply: 'I can't accept it.'

'You've no choice. Where will you hang it?'

Jemima felt absurdly vulnerable, absurdly on the defensive, without good reason. It was time she stood her ground. 'Tell me something.'

'Anything.'

'What do the numbers on your wrist mean? A tattoo must mean something. It's a date, isn't it?'

His face darkened. Something immeasurably sad yet fierce made a tumult in his eyes. 'The most important day in my life,' he said after a moment. 'I must not risk forgetting it, not ever, no matter how old and stupid I become.' He stared straight at her. 'It was the day my mother died.'

Jemima thought of that lovely face, preserved at its best on the back of a book — and preserved, it was all too apparent, in the son's stricken memory. She almost put out her hand to him; but something held her back.

When he spoke again, it was in his normal light, suggestive tone. 'Have dinner with me again.'

'Somewhere in walking distance. That car's in terminal collapse.'

'I'll take it home. Orestes can look at it for you.'

'It'll never get you there,' she protested.

'I have a way with machines. If not with women. The key?'

She hesitated, then took out the key and gave it to him. He bent as if to kiss her hand; but instead moved closer and kissed her cheek.

'You live in France,' said Jemima. 'Whereabouts?'

'In the country.'

'Your own place?'

'I stay with . . . with friends.' He was backing imperceptibly away, ready to put an end to this sort of conversation.

'In France where you live, you don't have a place,' said Jemima airily. 'In London where you visit, you have a house.'

'There's a reason.' He was at the door. 'I've always dreamed of marrying an English girl. I want to be ready.'

It was, she had to admit, not a bad exit line.

As he went out, a woman was standing outside with her finger ready to press the button. It was Mrs Westrop. She glanced back at the departing Nicky before accepting Jemima's invitation to come in.

'Nicky Karydas,' said Jemima. 'In shipping. I've not known him long.'

'It struck me I'd seen him before.' Dorothy Westrop stood for a moment glancing around the sitting room, then said bluntly: 'I came to apologise. For worrying you. I was silly. Just that when I heard about the old General it just . . . brought it all back in a rush. Jerry and me, and packing in the Army after all those years, and then that smallholding in France, and . . . I'm sorry. And you were just going out.' When Jemima waved her towards a chair, she shook her head. 'You're just going out.'

'How did he . . .?' Jemima stopped. 'No, you don't want to think about that.'

'It was a mystery. I was down in the village; he was moving hay in the barn. There was a hole in the roof so it all had to be at the dry end. It caught fire.'

'Fire? From a lamp, or something?'

'A lamp – in broad daylight?'

Jemima said carefully: 'Where was this? Nowhere near a place called Marie-la-Petite?'

'Not what you'd call near. Quite some miles away.'

'But you know it.'

'It's a beauty spot. Got one of those take-out-a-mort-gage-just-for-lunch restaurants.'

'La Maison aux Rossignols?'

'Oh, no,' said Mrs Westrop with a shaky laugh. 'That's not a restaurant. I think it's some sort of special hospital.'

'Special?'

'For some sort of special cases. Those who can afford it. We never really asked.'

All thoughts of returning to the office had fled from Jemima's mind. As soon as Mrs Westrop had left, she hurried out to the car. To find that it wasn't there – not even that scrapheap of a car the garage had lent her. Nicky had driven it off. She would have to grab a hire car. Jemima dashed back into the flat, telephoned urgently, and was fidgeting on the street doorstep when at last a moderately healthy vehicle was driven up for her.

One stop at a small shop in the western suburbs, and she was on her way to Stutworth.

Young Jemima accepted the compass with a gleam of greed but no show of gratitude.

'You're sure it's the best they had?'

'It's the only one you're going to get. And now,' said

Jemima, 'you said you knew who mixed petrol with the paraffin. Do you, or were you fibbing?'

'Of course I know.'

'Tell me.'

The child looked sneeringly up at her. 'Do I need to?'

'You need a good shaking.'

'Who do you think you're kidding? I know who was there the night before, and so do you.'

'Who?'

'I'd love a tent,' said young Jemima meaningly. 'That's what I really want. Are you going to buy me a tent?'

'Who *was* it?' Jemima could only just restrain herself from seizing the child by the throat.

'That car. You know all about it. It was parked there in the moonlight that night. Same place as when you came the other morning.'

'But which car? Whose car?'

'The same one. Your flashy Rolls, what else?' Young Jemima was virtually spitting the words into her face. '*Your* car was here. *You* were here. *You* mixed the petrol. *You* killed him.' She grinned evilly. 'And now what about that tent?'

It was time she got back to the office. Or, rather, it was long past time. Guthrie and Cherry greeted her with a fusillade of accusations.

'At two-thirty you were to meet Cy and the Chairman.'

'I forgot.'

'Cy was livid. Being stood up by a mere *entertainer*! Must have been a hell of a long lunch. Did he take you off in his private plane . . .?'

Jemima let the complaints rattle over her head. What was important was the stack of newspapers on her desk. She turned over the top one, gingerly opened a few drying pages, and then switched her attention to the obituaries.

There it was: a cropped version of the photograph on the back of the book she had bought, and the story of Irene Karydas, who had died in Nicosia. That brought her up sharp. Dying in Cyprus, not in Greece?

Jemima turned back to the news pages. One headline clawed at her attention. So did what came after.

AFTERMATH OF CYPRUS RIOT
Demand for Army Inquiry
16,000 books destroyed

As she read down the column, its terrible story was accompanied by other lines ringing in her head: *A day and night to be remembered and regretted.* Just as Major-General Ballister had jotted it down in those exercise-books. *Colonel Shore was completely in the right, and his men, including Captain Westrop . . .*

Cherry said in a hushed voice: 'Is it something bad? You look awful.'

'I feel awful.'

'Something came through while you were out. That Miss Glendenning — we did get word from Amalfi.'

'And?'

'She met your Nicky Karydas only once. And has no idea where he's to be found right now. Is that what you wanted to know?'

I'd sooner not have known any of it, thought Jemima. Sooner cancel out everything that has happened these last few days. And cancel dinner this evening. But that was impossible. The incredible truths were falling into place, and no matter what the danger, she knew she had to present those truths just the way they were.

She pushed away the newspapers and stood up. A few final details to check, so that this time she would be well prepared for Nicky Karydas, and then she would be on her way.

When Orestes opened the door of the house in Breck Place she said, before Nicky could appear: 'The other morning when you drove me to Stutworth . . .'

'Yes, madam?'

'Had you been there before? In the Rolls, the night before?'

He spoke levelly, but his right fist was clenching and unclenching. 'No, madam, I had not been there before.'

'Does *he* drive?'

'The master? Sometimes.'

Nicky was coming out to greet her, drawing her on towards the drawing room on the first floor, where a bottle of champagne waited in an ice bucket.

'My lovely Jemima.' His eyes took in her everyday two-piece. 'You didn't feel like dressing?'

'I've been too busy today. A new programme.'

'Poor darling. They ask too much of you.'

'A programme,' she said, 'about Cyprus.'

He was reaching for the champagne bottle. It was impossible to tell whether he did indeed hesitate for an instant, his fingers touching the neck of the bottle.

Orestes said, in an oddly harsh tone: 'Madam was asking if we knew a place called . . . what was it, madam?'

'Stutworth. Where my old friend died.'

For some reason avoiding his servant's accusing gaze, Nicky poured champagne into two glasses. 'I toast my fiancée. You forget sadness, forget about that fire –'

'Someone,' said Jemima, 'put petrol in his paraffin.'

With exaggerated flippancy Nicky jerked his head at Orestes. 'And she asks you if you did it, Orestes?'

'You know I didn't, sir.'

Nicky set his glass down and held out a car key. 'This

is what Orestes is good at. One car very slightly better than it was.'

As Orestes padded from the room, Nicky took Jemima's glass away and placed it beside his own. He bent to kiss her. She caught his hand, more firmly than he had expected, and slid the watch back.

'The seventeenth of September, 1955,' she said. 'The day your mother died, you told me. Mine was a bit later.' She took in the paintings, the hangings, the silk wallpaper and the shaded lighting of the room. 'Very good taste, Miss Mary Glendenning. Oh, yes, Nicky – I know it belongs to her.'

Only a brief twitch in the corner of his mouth revealed that he had been taken by surprise.

'So I borrow a friend's house?'

A friend who met you only once, thought Jemima: a friend who has no idea of your current whereabouts. She had little doubt that Orestes was clever with keys other than car keys, and skilled at getting in and out of places.

She said: 'Orestes has been with you a long time?'

'His mother was my mother's maid. We grew up together and he looks after me.'

'Looks after you at the House of Nightingales?'

Orestes had returned, standing in the doorway, his voice dying away in the middle of an announcement that dinner was served.

'A sort of hospital, I believe,' Jemima persisted.

'Not a hospital.' It was Orestes, not Nicky, who answered. 'A place where people rest.'

'Rich, nervous people with a lot to hide?' Before either of them could grope for a reply, she said: 'Which of you killed my friend? Which of you killed Major-General Ballister?'

'Oh, Jemima, how silly you –'

'Who has petrol?' she burst out. 'Cars have petrol, owners of cars have it, chauffeurs have plenty to spare. And at night, with the shed unlocked . . . Oh, it was one of you two. Why?'

'Please.' Orestes raised a warning hand. 'Please do not upset him.'

Jemima advanced on Nicky. 'Cyprus, seventeenth of September 1955.' It had become an incantation, a deadly challenge. 'Your mother's death. But what *else*? What did Cyprus have to do with either of you?'

Nicky flinched, trying to retain his suave, easy smile. 'My mother was in Cyprus on a visit. She took me. And her maid, and Orestes to keep me company while she worked. She was a writer, you know. A fine writer.'

'Yes, I know.' Jemima's breath rasped in her throat. 'Were you in Nicosia that night – the night of the fire? The night the books got burned? Sixteen thousand books?'

'Please.' Orestes was almost whimpering. 'I tried to warn you. Please, you go now. Get out and leave us.'.

Jemima's attention did not waver from Nicky Kary-das. 'You were there, the two of you. Kids – seven and ten, or thereabouts, right? Things very hairy, I'll bet. British out! Stones and bottles everywhere.'

'They pulled a Union Jack down and burned it on a soldiers' jeep.' Nicky was staring with narrowed eyes into a blazing past. With a pang Jemima saw his mother's features like a lovely ghost behind his own; but super-imposed was a rage which had gone beyond bitterness into uncontrollable madness. 'Your father's and Captain Westrop's soldiers.'

'My father and the Captain weren't even there until later. Only a patrol was there. Everyone else was at some RAF party, that much I've found out.'

'The patrol was *theirs*,' said Nicky implacably. 'That much *I* found out. The Captain's, the Colonel's, the General's. Orestes and I, we watched that night.'

'Watched? As the mob burst into the British Institute and set fire to it? The best library in the Mediterranean, destroyed by hooligans –'

'Orestes and I, we watched the fire. And laughed. We didn't know then.'

'Didn't know what?'

'My mother was in that building.' The horror of it hung in the air, as real to him today as it had been then. 'Researching in that best library of yours. That's why we were there, waiting for her. She was working late to get finished.'

'And the fire . . . she . . .?'

'Can she rest in heaven,' said Nicky, soft and steely, 'while those responsible go on living?'

Orestes tried to interpose himself, handing Jemima her shoulder bag. 'You go now.'

She ignored him. 'But after so long? And why us, when it was the Cypriots who set the fire anyway?'

'They weren't the enemy. You were. British bullies who drove them to it, drove them to madness. I was sorry to learn your father had already died in an accident. He was the one I couldn't have.' Nicky ran his hand wildly through his hair. 'Captain Westrop I found living in France, living so near. Oh, Jemima, I could not ignore such a sign from God! And the General – ah, he was a bonus. I didn't even know he was still alive until I started work on you. You led me to him.'

'But what part do I play? When you found my father was beyond your reach, how did I –'

'If you'd been plain and ordinary, I wouldn't have worked so hard. But I wanted to break your heart first. If you have a heart. They're not common in this country.

But to break at any rate one Shore . . . And it's the most perfect justice, you see. You are now the age my mother was when she died. You don't really think you have the right to live longer than she did?'

This time Jemima took her bag when Orestes offered it, and swung it over her shoulder. As she turned towards the door her neck began to prickle: she was sure Nicky was going to leap, to choke her or smash her head to a pulp, to drench her in petrol and set light to her.

'Leave her,' Orestes was saying pleadingly. 'Next time it won't be Rossignols. More trouble, and they won't be able to keep you.'

Jemima was tempted to stand her ground, to ask more questions, to wrap up every last little detail. But every nerve ending screamed of danger, her feet carried her forward, she was out of the room, out of the house – and there at the kerb was that pile of four-wheeled junk from the garage. Nicky, incredibly, had obeyed Orestes and let her go. It made no sense. She took out the key and hurried towards the car before he changed his mind.

A woman was getting out of a cab and approaching the house. She checked the number, rang the bell; and glanced curiously at Jemima. Above, the drawing room curtain twitched back and two heads were silhouetted against the light.

The woman stooped to the letter-box. 'Nicky! *C'est moi, Docteur Rolin*. Hélène!'

Jemima found when she reached it that the car door had not been properly shut. She would have expected Orestes to be more meticulous than that. Tugging it open, she slid in and groped for the ignition.

The key refused to engage. So much for Orestes' skill! Impatiently she got out again and stared up at the window, not wanting to risk going back into the house but not wanting to call either of them down.

The heads had disappeared from between the curtains.

Suddenly the woman who had called herself Doctor Rolin was being shoved unceremoniously aside. Nicky came bounding from the front door waving something in his hand, thrusting it towards Jemima, smiling as boyishly and eagerly as ever.

'It is a mistake. Jemima, my love, I am sorry.'

'Leave me alone.' She began to walk purposelessly away.

'So sorry. That fool Orestes, he give you the wrong key. He changes them, God knows why. Here is the right one.'

Faintly in the distance began the howl of a police siren. Nicky looked round, startled but not apprehensive until it began to come closer; not truly apprehensive until he saw Orestes and the woman doctor side by side, fatalistic, on the step.

'Orestes?' he faltered. 'You mean you . . . it is you, you have . . .?'

In the uncertain light Jemima saw Orestes' eyes widen. His hand went out as if he meant to lunge after Nicky. Then he froze. Jemima found herself stumbling past them and then stopping, unsure, afraid that Nicky might be setting off in pursuit of her.

She looked back, the useless car key still dangling from her finger. Nicky was sliding into the driving seat and leaning forward over the ignition.

The explosion struck up at the tall house fronts and bounced back across Breck Place. Flame gushed from the squat little car like a short-lived oil-well blowout – or a paraffin lamp fed with petrol.

So that fool Orestes, as Nicky had called him, had given her the wrong key deliberately, guessing or knowing what his employer had done to her car?

And Nicky, knowing full well which key was which . . .

Jemima ducked and turned her face away from the funeral pyre. It was the last, had to be the last, of that dreadful chain of murderous blazes: the pyres of poor dear old Major-General Ballister, of Captain Westrop whom she had never met but who had been doomed to play his part in the hideous tale, and of beautiful Irene Karydas.

Now – she choked back a tear, uncertain whose death she was most wretchedly lamenting – the Greek tragedy was at an end.

# A Model Murder

Mary Bernard had been pretty, which was why her face
and slim figure had appeared in so many advertisements
on the pages of so many magazines. She ceased being
pretty when she hit the pavement two storeys below the
window of the studio where she had been modelling.
The dark wayward hair that had been such an asset was
matted with blood, and her sulkily tempting mouth was
twisted into a final grimace of horror.

Nobody knew how she had come to fall. The photographer had been away only a couple of minutes,
moving his car before resuming their morning session,
and was on his way back up when the accident
happened. He heard nothing, saw nobody. It made no
sense. All it did make was a small headline in the evening
paper and a non-committal report at the end of a radio
news round-up.

The incident might never have come to Jemima
Shore's notice if she had not made an arrangement to
meet her friend Becky Robertson the next afternoon,
after lunch with an old flame who had surprisingly
shown signs of flickering again. Her mind was on their
puzzling conversation rather than on Becky's, but she
made the right sympathetic noises.

'She was on my case list about three years ago,' Becky

explained. 'The clinic put me on to her as some kind of misfit, after she'd tried to take an overdose. It wasn't as serious as it looked on paper: she told me she was just playing at it.'

'Jumping from a window isn't exactly playing at it,' observed Jemima.

'I don't understand it. I bumped into her a couple of months ago in Regent Street, and she seemed very happy. In with the Diana Boyle agency, pages in *Cosmo* and *Honey*, that sort of thing – suited her down to the ground. I can't help wishing she'd thought of me and just picked up the phone or something.'

Jemima tried to reassure her friend with the usual platitudes about not feeling too guilty, not trying to take responsibility for all the unavoidable personal tragedies in the world. Social workers like Becky, though, took their work and the worries of their clients very earnestly. She would fret for a long while yet.

When they parted, Jemima went off to see a bright young journalist who had recently come into her life. One pleasure being over – for the time being – she settled back in bed within the crook of his arm and decided to involve him in another – this time, the business which her chat with Becky had interrupted.

First of all she offered him a selective summary of her lunchtime discussion, and in spite of his jealously questioning stare did not, even to herself, make any comparisons between him and memories of Tom Amyas.

Lunching with a former lover could be nostalgic, nauseating, or suspicion-making. When a married man reappeared from one's past with an invitation to share a meal with him it could be interpreted as meaning either that his wife was away, or that he wanted to play on old affections in order to acquire information; or both. Since becoming an MP, Tom had risen to enviable heights by using his charm to manipulate things and people to serve his own best interests.

As he rose to greet her in the basement of the restaurant – a discreet distance from Westminster – he looked as handsome and self-assured as ever. The grooming of his iron-grey hair was nicely calculated to balance the youthfulness of his face against the gravity of his responsibilities. To clear the air, he admitted at once that his wife was out of town. He had been unable to accompany her because of this infernal referendum debate going on and on at awkward hours in the House. To make it equally clear that his invitation was not *that* kind of invitation – though he could not resist a hint that the two might not be incompatible – he said:

'I wanted to see you because I might have something for you. Something on that secret services project you were talking about.'

She reminded him that when she had in fact talked about it he had been stern and puritanical in his assurance that government information could not possibly be exposed on a television programme.

The waitress arrived, giving Jemima an awed, sidelong smile of recognition. Tom bristled slightly. Few people recognised their legislators so readily. When they had ordered, he went on: 'This time I've got something unofficial you might like to follow up.'

'Ah. What you mean is, you've got something you'd like dug over, but your delicate political hands mustn't get any mud on them – is that it?'

He acknowledged her shrewd assessment with a rueful nod. 'Let's just say that something's cropped up which would be tricky to handle in a routine way. I've had a letter from someone calling himself Colonel Curtis. Claims to have been in military intelligence: retired now, but wants to give me a lead on some high-level scandal he's got wind of. The Military won't authenticate him off-hand, and at this stage I don't want to get them too inquisitive by pushing too hard.'

'Why has he picked on you?'

'I have a small reputation,' said Tom with unconvincing diffidence, 'as a watchdog on the Parliamentary security committee.'

'You've replied to his letter?'

'Yes. All very melodramatic. You do get these Colonel X's and Admiral Y's popping out of the woodwork from time to time, so I'm playing it carefully. What I've suggested is that if he'll give his information to the media, I'll look for any evidence that might corroborate it, and take it from there.'

Jemima spooned up some of her avocado and prawns, reflecting on the way in which even the staunchest individualists could be moulded into the administrative pattern once they had reached a certain level. Outspoken as political candidates, promising fearless exposure of the ills of society and clean sweeps of shifty elements from the Civil Service and government ministries, they soon learned to adopt the same protective colouring and to shift responsibility on to other shoulders. If anyone was going to tread on a banana skin, it would not be Tom Amyas. He did not want to lose possible prestige by letting something important slip past him; but was not going to risk such prestige as he already possessed by striding too boldly into an inquiry which might go wrong.

'What do I have to do?' asked Jemima. 'Wait blindfold in a telephone box?'

'He doesn't want you to contact him direct. If you're agreeable, I'll give him your number at Megalith, and let him make the approach.'

In which case, thought Jemima, whether Tom approved or not she would have to let Cherry in on at least some of the story, otherwise she would assume it was just another of Jemima's wicked liaisons.

And she proposed, for practical reasons, to let the latest of those wicked liaisons in on as much of the story as would make him useful to her.

David Cullen was a rather lovely young man with unruly sandy hair and deceptively innocent blue eyes. They had met at a rather boring party, full of radical ideologists in camouflage jackets, holding forth about the monopolistic elements of the international power structure and drinking lager out of cans. Within twenty minutes they had left together; and within a week had come together several more times in quick succession. It was difficult, in his distracting company, to sort out coolly and rationally just how much to tell him. Come to that, it was difficult to know just how much there would be to tell anybody in the end. Retired army colonels were pretty thick on the ground – and some of them were pretty thick elsewhere. As for the ones who claimed to have secrets to sell, how many of them were simply trying to boost their egos and re-live past glories by talking big? And how many were likely to be traitors, defectors, men with rankling grudges, spreading dissent for the sheer hell of it?

As an investigative journalist who had touched on a few political and espionage themes in her programmes, Jemima suspected that this Colonel Curtis would prove to be what was known in the trade as a non-admitted person. This meant that officially he did not exist. Any accusation he might make would be smartly denied, and records produced to back up the denial. Once you started prodding into the state clockwork, you soon found yourself in Alice-in-Wonderland territory. Tom Amyas was all too well aware of that, which was why he had so deftly given Jemima the job of testing the mechanism.

When she had selected as much as she thought it politic for David to know, he sprawled back on his pillow and said: 'It all sounds a bit hazy to me. What do you expect me to do about it?'

'You're pretty handy with a camera as well as with words, aren't you?'

'Flattery will get you anywhere.'

'If I give you a ring, could you be around to take a few pictures without being spotted?'

'I think I could rise to the occasion. Which reminds me . . .'

The occasion was not long in coming. Colonel Curtis telephoned the office when she was out, and gave Cherry a brusque, matter-of-fact message. He made an appointment to meet Jemima at her flat this coming Thursday afternoon. There was no question of his being seen entering or leaving the Megalith building. Furthermore, he would permit no cameras. The meeting was to be strictly on a one-to-one basis or not at all.

So there would have to be a tape running in the flat, and a hidden mike. If David could take a few stills of the man on his way in and out, Jemima could keep them in reserve and maybe use them with a voice-over from the tape: always assuming that there was anything worth repeating, and enough of it to form the basis of a worthwhile programme.

'All right,' she agreed. 'Phone him and tell him –'

'We're not to phone him,' said Cherry. 'He'll ring to confirm that the date and time suit you. End of message. Over and out.'

It was growing more like an exasperating spy thriller every minute. There had better be a good pay-off.

On Thursday afternoon Jemima sat by her window,

not too blatantly peering out but able to detect any movement in the street. A car stopped briefly three doors down, then went on its way. David, arriving with a good half-hour to spare, had patiently settled himself behind an ornamental espalier in a garden across the road. A lone cyclist wobbled past, round the corner towards Holland Park Avenue.

Right on the dot a taxi drew up. The man who got out was burly and heavily deliberate in his movements. He wore a tweed cap and a fawn-coloured trench coat, its hue matched by the sort of clipped moustache which Jemima thought had gone out of fashion half a century ago.

She was ready to let him in the moment the bell rang, but opened the door very slowly so that he would be kept on the step for a moment or two. His handshake was hard and brief, his eyes hard and steady save for one twitch towards the other side of the road.

'I see you were prepared for me, Miss Shore. I imagine he's got enough material by now, so may I come in?'

Jemima gulped as she closed the door behind him.

In the sitting room he cast a knowing eye at the furniture and at the vase of flowers on the table. 'I expect you've got a tape recorder tucked away somewhere. But I'd like it understood that any record you keep of this meeting is for you and me only.'

'Would you like a drink, Colonel?'

'A whisky, if you have it.'

When they were seated, Jemima tried to reassert herself. She was not accustomed to being taken off guard like that or stared at so disconcertingly.

'If you don't object to photographs and tape recorders,' she said, 'why did you object to a full-scale interview?'

'I've no wish to be involved in the television circus. My only desire is to make known certain facts and have them followed up. I can appreciate Mr Amyas's reasons for putting me on to a go-between such as yourself, but I'm not going to be put up as a personality on your screen.'

'If you want any co-operation at all, Colonel, you've got to put yourself up as *something*. I mean, if you expect to be credible –'

'My credibility is irrelevant.' He gave her a thin, curt smile. 'For what it's worth, however, I was commissioned not long after this last War. Joined the Army as a boy in '42, came back from Korea as a Major. Served in Berlin and then the Middle East.' His smile mellowed slightly. 'It might interest you to know I remember your father there. You have his looks, if I may say so. Don't think you were with them at the time.'

'I was at boarding school in Sussex. I was just going up to Cambridge when they were killed in that accident.'

'You were their only child?' There was a strange melancholy in his voice.

'Yes. I don't think my mother wanted to inflict an Army life on me or any more . . .' She broke off. 'Is this your dossier, or mine?'

He took another sip from his whisky, and snapped out: 'Are you familiar with the name of Richard Clarendon?'

'Something to do with the Foreign Office, isn't he? One of the Whitehall mandarins.'

'Until very recently, Miss Shore, Clarendon had a mistress – a girl half his age.'

Jemima shrugged. Whatever Clarendon had to do with this business, a mistress half his age hardly qualified him for the *Guinness Book of Records*. If Curtis was trying for some personal reason to make a political scandal out of it, he was as old-fashioned as his moustache.

'A pretty girl,' the Colonel went on. 'Pretty enough to be working as a model here in London, and doing quite well for herself.'

Again this was nothing out of the way. 'So she's a model, like a lot of other attractive mistresses. Nothing new in that.'

'I agree. But not all of them end up silenced for it, Miss Shore. By which I mean murdered.'

'This girl . . . her name?' Jemima had a creepy feeling that she knew it already.

She was right. In Colonel Curtis's opinion, the verdict of misadventure on Mary Bernard was nonsense. She had been killed to shut her up. He had no evidence that would stand up in court, but he knew. Others knew it, too, but he would not say who those others were: only that the full background to the story was being deliberately withheld from the press. He had wanted Tom Amyas to institute a secret inquiry and bring out the truth. Now he understood that Miss Jemima Shore, Investigator, had the facilities for such an exposé. His expression showed that he doubted it. Tom Amyas's wariness had probably struck him as being a rebuff, and now perhaps he was preparing to make what in his own terms could be regarded as a tactical withdrawal.

By now, though, he had aroused Jemima's own hunting instincts. After he had left, she summoned David indoors and pored over the prints he rushed through for her in an improvised dark-room – her bathroom. They revealed nothing more than she had already seen: the weathered, commanding features, the crisp moustache, and the tight lips which had started to tell her something and then refused to tell her enough.

It was impossible to guess who he worked for, if indeed he still did any work at all. The whole thing might be a calculated leak, unofficial and indirect, so that nobody in high office would get his hands dirty. Any dirt there might be was left for Jemima Shore.

Oddly, she was left with something else: the merest glimpse of something vulnerable, something sad, behind the Colonel's military manner.

She wished she had asked Becky more questions about Mary Bernard, but at the time the name had been of no apparent relevance. Now it was time to pick up the threads again.

Becky could not offer much more. She knew nothing of any flat-mate in whom Mary might have confided, and Jemima allowed herself the thought that with Clarendon in regular attendance the girl would have been happier without a flat-mate.

'But there was one girl with her, once when I met her,' Becky recalled. 'I have an idea she was the one who helped Mary get a foot in the door at that agency. Jenny something – a blonde girl, quite tall.'

'Do you still have the files on the Bernard girl? Family background, that sort of thing?'

'They're . . . well . . .'

'Confidential?'

'Yes. Really they are.'

Confidentially, thought Jemima sourly, it takes a lot of confidence to push a girl out of a window to her death and expect to get away with it.

It needed at least the same amount of confidence to go out there and prove what happened, and who made it happen. Jemima knew her own symptoms: knew she was too deeply committed, in spite of the sketchiness of the hints and theories, to give up now.

She went to see Clive Gartrell, the photographer who had known how to shoot Mary Bernard in the right light, in the right poses, for the right market.

He recognised her at once. His eyes gleamed with assumed lust which he hoped would flatter her. Jemima guessed at the assumption, discarded the likelihood of anything interesting developing from it, and was by now sated with the flattery to which all television presenters were subjected. She said: 'I wonder if I could talk to you for a moment about Mary Bernard?'

He reacted with weary resignation, sauntering back across his studio and waving her to follow him in.

'I might as well open a bleeding waxworks and forget about taking pictures. All right, what is it this time? A half-hour special on decadent model's wicked life? Or do you want to sell me some windows people can't fall out of, for a double-glazing commercial?'

'I just want to find out whether her death made any sense to you.'

'Nobody's death makes any sense to me, sweetheart. Look, Mary Bernard, she made about four hundred in a good week, and now she's dead? That make any sense? I worked with her, all right, but that was all. I didn't screw her, just in case you're going to ask.'

'I wasn't.'

'The law did.'

'If you didn't, who did?'

His shoulders drooped with contempt rather than exhaustion. 'Whoever it was, he'd have to be well loaded. Expensive tastes she had. The smell of Grecian 2000 was what she really favoured.'

'Can you think of anyone in particular that she talked about?'

'Herself,' said Gartrell flatly. 'All models do a lot of that. About themselves or each other. What the hell else have they got to talk about?'

'Would she have talked a lot to Jenny, do you think?'

The hunch of his shoulders grew taut. 'You know

Jenny, too? I shall start having my suspicions about your tastes, in a minute.'

'Why?'

'Well, Jenny Stone's the sort of lady who'll try anything once, isn't she? As you'd know damn well if you ...' He leered, then snarled in his thin Birmingham accent: 'But you don't know her, do you? Just what are you after?'

'Did you like Mary?'

He sighed. 'Sure. A brain like candy floss, but I liked her. And now I'm trying to get it off my back. A suicide on your doorstep isn't exactly inspiring, you know.'

'What if it wasn't suicide?'

He was looking her straight in the face, and he was pale and there was no affectation of weariness or flip humour now. 'Listen. I had the police all over here for a week, like woodworm specialists. After they'd breathed on every lens and tried to find some porn in my negatives, they decided on misadventure. You don't get me on any TV crap about murder! Now can I get on with some work?'

Jemima had had a tiring, grubby day: grubby not just in the dirt you acquired simply by driving or walking from one place to another in London, but sordid in all its implications. A bath was essential. Late in the evening she crawled into a liberal helping of scented foam and lay gratefully back.

After ten minutes, further bits of dirt surfaced in her mind and she reached for the telephone.

Tom Amyas was at home. She did not bother to ask politely if his wife was back yet, and if it was all right to talk. He had started this, he could cope with any consequences. She said: 'I've got a feeling there's an unofficial leak in the ship of state, Tom. Your Colonel friend says Richard Clarendon was having an affair with a young model. Yes' – as he tried to interrupt – 'fine, that's what I said to myself, too. Best of British luck and all that. But the model happened to drop from a window, and our friend says it wasn't an accident. Your man from the Ministry, his little mistress Mary ... and murder. Don't you think you ought to talk to Clarendon direct, instead of leaving me to scrabble round the edges?'

His answer was so evasive that she treated it as it deserved, by hanging up in the middle.

Upon which her doorbell rang.

Jemima tried to ignore it, but after a few more insistent shrills she grabbed her bathrobe, kicked some flecks of foam from her toes, and went out.

David beamed. 'Did I interrupt something?'

'Yes. I was in the bath.'

'I'm perfectly prepared to discuss the matter in the bath if that's what you –'

'This is not a civilised hour to call on people. Some of us have to get up and work in the morning.'

He winced. 'What a nasty habit.'

Inevitably she let him in. No reason not to let him in to her sitting room again, when she had let him into so many of her secrets.

'I thought you should know' – he was eyeing not so much her bathrobe as the patches which the robe failed to conceal – 'that a friend of mine with his ear to the ground –'

'And *you* talk about nasty habits?'

'My friend,' he persevered, 'tells me that your chum Clarendon is involved in some devious bargaining with one of the OPEC countries right now.'

'So?'

'So it occurred to me that maybe the girl you're interested in was summoning up the breath to blow the whistle on him at just the wrong moment.'

Someone of Clarendon's status would be capable of having his little bit of stuff done away with, just like that, because of matters of state? What a state, thought Jemima, flinching away from the mere idea. Yet she had in her career had ample evidence that the rulers of every nation had done that and worse. Termination with prejudice, the Americans called it. That way it didn't sound like murder.

'But why,' she ventured, 'should the Colonel leak a stinker like that, just now?'

'Maybe the Military don't like whatever the deal is. Maybe the Colonel has some ancient chip on his shoulder to match his crown or whatever, and lumbered that same shoulder with an urge to discredit Clarendon.'

'The War Office stabbed Westminster in the back?'

'I think they call it the Ministry of Defence nowadays, duckie.'

'You could fool me.'

She said it brashly, but by now was resolved not to be fooled. There might not be a viable programme in this, but there was certainly something; and if she intended to thrash it out, Megalith's resources might as well contribute.

Next morning she gave Cherry enough instructions to keep her busy for a good two hours. Cherry, as ever, proved her worth by coming up with answers within a mere hour and a half.

The model girl Jenny Stone was with the Boyle agency just as Mary Bernard had been. It was a three-year-old agency which had blossomed fast and not been nipped by the frost of the recession. The Boyle set-up did a fair amount of work for clients abroad as well as for the glossiest home-grown magazines and classiest commercials, and had shown a flair for finding new faces.

Diana Boyle was an ex-model who had dominated the scene in the 'sixties and now knew how best to deploy a younger generation from her office in Maddox Street.

'Behind which,' Cherry revealed, 'is a money man called Seyid Beirun.'

'Now, there's a name to conjure with. An Arab oil sheikh?'

'Iranian. Took up British residency after the fall of the Shah, and does well enough to run a house in Mayfair and another in Sussex. He buys and sells property, makes contacts as fast as a three-pin plug, and owns a restaurant called the Arabian Nights.'

'Sheep's eyes and belly dancers?'

'I wouldn't know,' said Cherry; 'my salary doesn't run to that kind of thing.'

'On the subject of contacts, did you get hold of Jenny Stone?'

'Not yet.'

'Let's split it up right now. I'm expecting a call from Tom Amyas. Then I'll pursue the Jenny angle, while you pay a visit to the Boyle agency. Give them a line about a fashion programme we're doing, modelling and the lot, buttons and bows and strains and stresses, and see how Miss Boyle reacts. You never know, she might offer you a job.'

'You never know,' said Cherry in a fine parting shot: 'I might take it.'

Cherry's acid retorts demonstrated, month in and month out, more genuine affection and loyalty than many a sickly compliment Jemima had been offered.

The report she brought back led, unfortunately, nowhere. Diana Boyle had assumed the correct expression of sorrow when Mary Bernard's name came up; the right gleam of interest when Cherry hinted at a possible programme on the modelling profession and the stresses behind the glamour; and cool unhelpfulness when Cherry mentioned Jenny Stone. Yes, Jenny had known Mary and worked with her, but she was out of the country right now on a campaign for some big French and German advertisers. No, she was sorry, it was not their policy to divulge the girls' home telephone numbers. No, she was not sure when Jenny would be back. All she could promise was to ask her to ring Miss Shore at Megalith when she did return.

'The only thing I did manage to bring away with me,' said Cherry shamelessly, 'was a publicity handout showing some of the agency's top models. Just happened to be lying on a table in reception.' She flipped over a couple of glossy pages to show a girl with a wide mouth and a fine, thin face, her hair piled extravagantly up into a veritable explosion of blonde fire. 'That's Jenny Stone, for all the good it does us.'

She confessed to having had a hunch that Miss Boyle had been waiting only for her to quit the premises before phoning somebody and setting off a whole carillon of alarms: just a hunch, that was all.

Jemima would have backed most of Cherry's hunches against the sworn statements of any ten other witnesses. This did not please her all that much.

She summoned Tom Amyas to another lunch. He was none too pleased, either.

'It's true,' he said as soon as the bottle of Pichon Lalande had been decanted and the carafe set on the table between them. 'Clarendon was having an affair with that girl.'

'So our spy was telling the truth.'

'Clarendon denied it at first. Then I got a call from the Foreign Secretary this morning. Apparently the intelligence services have known about it almost from the word go. Curtis was way out of line in telling you, though.'

'And who put him on to me in the first place?' she asked with some asperity.

He evaded that one. 'I shouldn't think you'll hear any more from him.'

'They've admitted to him as genuine?'

'They could hardly dodge it, once he'd let the cat out of the bag.'

'I wonder why he did it? But the real question,' said Jemima firmly, 'is whether Clarendon was responsible for her death.'

'Not as far as any prosecution is concerned, it seems.'

His attempt to draw a line under the whole thing and write it off made Jemima just about as uneasy as Tom looked. If Curtis had stuck his neck out to expose Clarendon, he must have had a good reason. And if the powers that be had decided to hush it up, probably chucking the Official Secrets Act at anyone who probed too deeply, then there must be a reason for that, too.

She said: 'It's a cover-up.'

'Of course. But it's a cover-up of . . . well . . . an indiscretion, not a murder case.'

'That's a politician's stance, Tom. I'm not a politician.'

'You're not a Special Branch detective, either,' he said grouchily. 'All right, so Curtis somehow got to know about the affair. So did half a dozen other people, and none of them have shouted murder, have they? The verdict was misadventure, and everyone's cleaving to that.'

'Except the Colonel and Becky Robertson,' said Jemima, 'and me.'

She was far from soothed when Becky came up with the news that all her old records on the subject had disappeared from the office files. She had checked as discreetly as possible in case somebody else had taken them out for a case study; but as far as the department was concerned, Mary Bernard had simply ceased to exist.

It had to be somebody with enough power to go through Civil Service records when they felt like it. If Colonel Curtis's superiors had wanted that file, it would presumably have been handed to them on a plate.

Jemima was getting that familiar prickly sensation down the back of her neck. The accompanying sensation was one of disbelief – a growing doubt as to whether Mary's death had really had anything to do with the brass hats or Whitehall bowlers after all. Whatever his motive for approaching Tom Amyas, Colonel Curtis has assumed that the girl was killed because of her affair with Clarendon; and the authorities were covering tracks like a dump truck loaded with high-grade mud. Yet Tom had sounded sincere in that 'indiscretion, not murder' line of his, and somehow Jemima found herself dabbling with the notion of another motive altogether. She remembered her unsatisfactory interview with Clive Gartrell, and Cherry's similarly unsatisfactory one with Diana Boyle. Both had been stalling. Neither of them wanted her to get close to Jenny Stone.

It looked as though she would have to start retracing her steps: back to Mr Gartrell, for instance.

She had swung in to the kerb and was about to get out when the door below the studio window opened and Clive Gartrell came out: came out in a hurry, hustled from behind. With him was a tall blonde girl in a gleaming black jacket and black leather pants tucked into high boots. As her head swung to protest to the man holding her arms behind her back, Jemima caught a glimpse of the wide mouth and high cheekbones she had seen in the photograph of Jenny Stone.

Three men were bunched around Jenny and Clive

Gartrell: two dark-skinned toughs, and one slimmer, bearded man in a grey suit. He might have been an Arab diplomat – or, thought Jemima dourly, an Iranian entrepreneur who had just had some bad news.

The girl and the photographer were hustled towards a large black Mercedes. There was no polite nonsense about holding the door open and bowing Jenny in: she was thrust unceremoniously in, with Gartrell following.

Jemima let the car move off and reach the next corner before she edged her white Mercedes out in pursuit of the black one. A flicker of movement in her mirror tugged at her attention. Was that Range Rover the same one she had noticed behind her a couple of times already, yesterday and today?

She was getting jumpy. In any case it was the car ahead that mattered.

Traffic was thick enough to tax all her skills in tailing the black saloon. She dared not risk any impetuous overtaking in case this drew attention to her presence. The best she could hope for was to keep no more than two other vehicles between her and her quarry.

They seemed to be heading for Camden Town. At one set of traffic lights the saloon pulled out and signalled to turn right. Jemima left it to the last minute before swinging out and following, to find herself in a perilously empty street. She was too exposed. On impulse she made for a narrow lane between two decrepit buildings, and parked. When she ventured back to the corner, it was to see Jenny Stone and Clive Gartrell being rushed up the steps of a bridge. At first she thought there must be a railway beneath, but when she moved closer she could smell the canal even before she saw it.

There was a solid iron division along the middle of the walkway. Jemima slid along one side, measuring her pace to match the clanging footsteps of the others on the far side.

At the end she paused to let them descend to a desolate cul-de-sac, lined by abandoned buildings. When they had reached a set of double doors and the bearded man had opened one, she emerged on to the steps – to cannon into a man with a leather wind-cheater and a jauntily set beret.

'Oh!' The breath burst from her not because of the collision but out of a panic she at once fought down. He was not one of the group; only a youngish stranger with a quizzical grin. 'I'm sorry,' she said, and he raised a hand in casual salute.

She let him go on his way before venturing to cross the road and look at the large building from the cover of a peeling, sagging doorway.

The doors were those of what had once been public swimming baths. Tilting from one wall was a sign saying 'Acquired', though it was difficult to imagine what it could possibly have been acquired for.

The Iranian – she knew now, was sure now – came out suddenly with one of his muscle-men, and hurried back over the bridge.

Jemima heard the sound of their Mercedes starting up again. When they had gone, she stared at those doors, tempted to go straight in . . . and then what? Her every instinct was to tackle trouble head on: all except that one instinct of self-preservation, which told her that the best thing was to call for help, and quickly.

Tom Amyas had started all this, but he was hardly the type to come dashing to her rescue. She had no time to waste listening to excuses about division bells and the need for an MP to keep his fingers whiter than white.

She went to the open end of the cul-de-sac, and on the far side of a patch of waste ground saw a telephone box. Miraculously, it had not been vandalised.

David Cullen said incredulously: 'Kidnapped? Both of them?'

'They weren't brought here for a swimming gala.'

'You're sure you know who –'

'It has to be that Seyid Beirun, the one whose finger Cherry found in every pie.'

'Come again?'

'David, there's no time for jokes. Who else could it be? I talk to Clive Gartrell about Jenny Stone, Cherry talks to Diana Boyle about Jenny Stone, they both clam up . . . and next thing you know they've been comparing notes, and their rich Iranian chum doesn't like it and hustles Gartrell and the girl off. They're involved in something, and Mary Bernard knew it. That's the real reason she was killed.'

'You won't get the law to pull a man in on your say-so. They'll need some kind of testimony.'

'It's waiting,' said Jemima impatiently, 'in the swimming bath.'

'With some big strong gorilla on the diving board?'

'I was relying on a big, strong gorilla-tamer like you.'

'Now, wait a minute. Taking photographs is one thing. Playing Clint Eastwood's another. He wins because it's in the script.'

'We'll cheat. Get some bananas on the way.'

'This is crazy.'

But he was on his way.

The door creaked open. Jemima went through – two paces behind David. He ought to have been carrying a blackjack or at the very least a length of lead piping. Instead there was a takeaway carton in his left hand, as if he had obeyed her instructions and stocked up with bananas.

They picked their way over fallen plaster and fragments

of unidentifiable upholstery towards a long, damp corridor which led to the pool. Once there had been oval panes of glass in the upper part of the swing doors at the end. Now one gaped wide, the other was patched up with tattered cardboard.

Jemima came up alongside David and squinted through at an angle. There was the wide, empty trough of what had once been the swimming bath, littered with what looked like chunks of collapsing ceiling. Along one side, cubicles had the air of long-neglected public lavatories. Just inside the doors was the entrance to a boiler-room.

David braced himself, and went through to the edge of the drained pool.

The heavy who had been left on duty came blundering out of the boiler-room.

'What do you think you –'

'From Mr Beirun,' said David ingratiatingly. He peeled the lid from the takeaway carton, and a steaming hot smell of rich curry wafted over the cold dampness of the tiles. 'For you, dinnertime, M'sieur.'

The man glared, but lowered his head a fraction to inhale the aroma.

David's hand came up briskly. The food went up into the man's face: into his eyes and nose rather than his mouth. There was a choking splutter of rage. David let go of the carton, swung to one side, and swung a haymaker. Big as he was, the heavy seemed to float out into space. There was nothing else to float on: he hit the cracked, pale green bottom of the pool with a sickening thud; but was scrambling to his knees, panting, reaching for his gun.

David plunged into the flimsy shelter of a cubicle. One bullet scoured the woodwork of the lintel, another screeched along the tiles.

Jemima said, in what she recognised as a crazily schoolmistressy tone: 'Drop it! D'you hear me?'

Crouched and venomous, the man was bringing the gun up slowly, taking his time and preparing to fire straight at her.

'Hold it! Freeze!'

A young man was falling from the gallery above – falling and landing neatly on the man with the gun. The two of them heaved up, tangled for a moment, and then the newcomer was efficiently lashing the gunman's hands behind his back. He favoured Jemima with the quizzical grin she had seen once already today.

Colonel Curtis appeared at her elbow. 'I wouldn't play that game too often, Miss Shore,' he said with a grudging, unmilitary note of admiration in his voice.

'I wasn't banking on it as a career,' she said shakily.

Colonel Curtis glanced at David. 'I trust you'll forgive the intrusion.'

'I bloody well will.' David emerged cautiously from the cubicle. 'Still, he didn't go much on the Vindaloo, did he?'

Jemima stared down at the young man and his captive. 'You've been having me followed,' she accused Curtis. 'All the time. That man . . .'

'I had to find out, you see, and my hands have been a little tied lately. It seems I was right about the murder but wrong about the motive, doesn't it? You dug up rather more than expected, Miss Shore.'

He led the way into the boiler-room. Gartrell and Jenny Stone were tied to the complex of piping and stop-cocks. David made a move towards them, but the Colonel put a restraining hand on his arm.

Jemima said: 'Jenny. It is Jenny Stone, isn't it?' When the girl, slumped forward, summoned up a nod, she went on: 'What's it all about? Did Beirun kill Mary?'

Gartrell twisted in a vain endeavour to wrench himself free. 'Listen, we're no part of that. You want to nail Beirun, OK. We're in a bloody mess, but we didn't kill anybody, right?'

'So what were you up to?'

Gartrell relapsed into sullen silence.

Jemima turned back to Jenny. 'Let's have the truth, and I'll go to the police with you. I'll tell them all about this and say you wanted to talk. You did want to, didn't you?'

Jenny nodded again.

'Oh, what the hell,' said Gartrell. 'We were running smack for him. Bringing it in from Germany or France.'

'Smack?'

'Heroin,' said Colonel Curtis softly.

'Beirun had the connection in Iran, they'd get it to the Continent, we'd pick it up. Diana Boyle knew the set-up, so she booked us together whenever there was work there. Nasty, but it paid a lot more than snapshots.'

'And Mary found out?'

'She came with us about six weeks ago,' Jenny whispered. 'She saw me with it in the hotel, so I told her. I thought she'd be cool. She was. Too cool, the stupid bitch.'

'Dizzy tart,' said Gartrell vindictively. 'She only threatened to pull the plug on Beirun if he didn't pay her some massive amount she asked for. Big mouth. Said she wasn't scared of him. She knew some big noise in the government who'd walk all over him. But you don't threaten a guy like Beirun. What did she think she was going to do – phone the House of Commons?'

'She was killed in your studio,' said Jemima sombrely. 'How did Beirun manage that?'

Gartrell jerked his head at the young man hauling the crumpled heavy past the doorway. 'Ask him. He's a specialist.'

'I think it's time we called the police,' said Jemima.

'Now wait a minute. I said we didn't kill her –'

'And you said you were going to talk to them for us,' whined Jenny.

'Yes, I'll do just that,' said Jemima. 'I'm going to tell them you were smuggling smack.'

Curtis had thrust his face close to Clive Gartrell's. 'You tried to drag her into that filth,' he said. 'You . . . heroin . . . filth. I hope you . . . I hope . . .'

His face worked for a moment, then he turned and strode after his side-kick.

'Colonel!' Jemima called. 'Colonel, what was Mary Bernard to you?'

But there was only the distant thump of the outer doors.

Tying up the last loose ends, Jemima strolled in the park with Becky, who first of all refused to believe in the violence of what had happened, and then wiped away a tear and shook her head over the memory of poor Mary Bernard. The girl had not had any idea what she was up against.

Neither, thought Jemima, had the other two; but they knew now. The verdict and sentence on charges of smuggling, conspiracy, and accessories after the fact would not be lenient. Still it would not be severe enough to satisfy Colonel Curtis. As for Seyid Beirun, the only pity was that Devil's Island was not available as his future residence.

'One thing I've been waiting to tell you,' said Becky as they took the path between the flower-beds. 'About your Colonel. Nothing definite, but I thought you'd like to know.'

'Indeed I would. What have you found?'

'After that file went missing I looked up some of my own case notes. Scribbled in a notebook as I went along, you know the sort of thing. I found some on a chat I'd had with Mary about her family and things. I'd forgotten that she was adopted, right after she was born. She never met her real parents, but her foster-mother once told her that it was all some forbidden affair in a well-to-do colonial family. Tea plantations and all that, you know.'

'Yes,' said Jemima pensively, 'I know.'

'They said her father had been an Army officer, stationed abroad. Put two and two together, and it would explain why he stepped forward, wouldn't it? What do you think?'

'I think we ought to go and have a coffee somewhere,' beamed Jemima. 'And I think you'd have a great future running an investigative TV programme.'

# Death à la Carte

The restaurant did not so much stand on the river bank as recline on it. Stretching itself luxuriously, it extended one graceful wing to enclose a patio with a tinkling fountain, and gazed through the languid eyes of its spacious windows upon the gardens and lawn sloping down towards the water. Inside, the décor was chic and expensive, the tables aglow with silver place-settings and sprigs of flowers.

The food, too, was out of the ordinary. As the proprietor explained devoutly to Jemima Shore, he was an expert in his chosen field. He was bringing a new *frisson* to the English palate. Here in these beautiful surroundings it was his mission to devise beautiful dishes for the beautiful people, connoisseurs so rarely catered for in so-called fashionable restaurants. The Roland Routier establishment was creating its own fashion in succulent, delicious, inimitable food.

'Such as tripe?' said Jemima, studying the ornately printed menu with which he had reverently presented her.

'Tripe,' breathed Routier. 'Ah, yes. And also there is our *foie gras* in a waistcoat, our sweetbreads, our hearts' – he touched his chest dreamily – 'not to mention our kidneys.'

Jemima would not have dreamed of mentioning his or anyone else's kidneys.

She had already had a preliminary report on the kitchen and its products and people. Preparing a documentary on offal and its high-protein merits, she had sent her ebullient secretary up-river to inspect the premises so that they could balance one style of cookery against another. 'Cheap nosh for the urban peasant,' Cherry had ungraciously said on setting off, 'or overpriced nosh for rich twits.' As a punishment she had been directed to bend over steaming pots and, in the course of duty, inhale the smells of unmentionable parts of various animals' anatomies.

Her report was nevertheless objective. She summed up the staff she had met with crisp accuracy. Georgie, head cook under Routier, had an unidentifiable foreign accent but a quite identifiable flair for his work. He almost sang when describing the ivory suet he was beating out around an ox kidney; and raged contemptuously about everybody else 'cooking with crap packets' instead of the real thing. Once or twice Cherry had ducked as he sharpened a knife on a butcher's steel and flourished it dramatically. He caressed a pig's head, boasted of four generations of culinary genius in his family, and ended his harangue with the scornful shout that 'Routier, he cannot poach an egg on me!' His assistant cook, Colin, was keen but slapdash, and much given to holding forth in a high Geordie voice. Then there were three trimly dressed waitresses, all pretty, as befitted the seductive atmosphere of the restaurant – one of them very dark and very Italian with fiery eyes.

'Sounds as if it'll make a really colourful feature,' said Guthrie Carlyle with that whimsical scepticism which he so often applied to programme ideas threatening to get out of hand. 'Olive-eyed Italian passion, dark brown offal all over the plates ... and blood everywhere.'

'Blood?'

'Don't tell me they don't make their own black puddings in the pig-sty on the estate?'

Further fantasies had been interrupted by the arrival of Dennis Jones, a tall, gangling man with a fearsome handshake and a lopsided grin which managed to be both brash and wary. In spite of his unglamorous name, he was the brother of Roland Routier.

'Mr Jones' – Jemima consulted her background notes – 'trained for the Rome Olympics on a diet of offal and onions.'

Guthrie remained unimpressed. 'Remarkable.'

'And won a gold medal.'

Before Guthrie could offer another indifferent shrug, Dennis Jones had grabbed him and lifted him high into the air.

'Mister World, Tokyo, '66.' Dennis set the alarmed Guthrie gently back on the edge of the desk. 'Mighty Muscles, Los Angeles, '67.'

Jemima smiled. 'Guthrie's into health foods at the moment. He says it's carnivores who cause all the trouble in the world. Too many calories make you want to go out and murder people.'

Dennis Jones grinned that same crooked grin.

For some reason he looked less self-assured when there were just Jemima and himself together, driving out of London. As she freed the Mercedes from the worst of the traffic and put her foot down, she began to ask questions and to slot the answers into her mind, ready for extraction if the programme needed them. Some of his answers were brusque and off-hand, and sometimes he looked away as if resenting having to collaborate on this project.

'Why did your brother change his name to Routier? I mean, I'm assuming *you* didn't change your name to Jones?'

'When we went into the restaurant business he felt he needed that sort of label.'

'I fancy I've read about him in the gossip columns,' Jemima prompted. 'The Casanova of the *haute cuisine* . . .'

'The customers enjoy it.'

'The Gallant of the Galley,' she quoted.

He was scowling at the road ahead. 'Roland is a serious cook and a happily married man, Miss Shore.'

'How disappointing.'

'Not at all. Everything the way it ought to be. Monica – that's his wife – runs our shops in town. She has nothing to do with the restaurant except that she buys the flowers.'

'What's Mrs Routier like?'

'Good background in the catering trade. Knows how to get people to do things right. God help 'em if they step out of line. And she's given Roland terrific support, right from the beginning. So whatever you read in the papers, you can forget it.'

It was virtually an order, not a comment.

They came over a ridge and were dazzled by sunlight striking across the curve of the river below. A faint haze shimmered between the trees and along the top of a meticulously clipped hedge.

'Take a left here,' said Dennis.

Jemima turned the car in between two impressive gateposts and on to a long drive, sweeping up to the restaurant's main entrance. As if alerted by some sentry on the slope down which she had just driven, a welcoming committee was lined up on the steps: two cooks, three waitresses, and a suave-looking man as tall as

Dennis Jones and with a slightly more ingratiating, calculating version of Dennis's features. His chef's hat looked rakish rather than practical.

A handsome woman in her mid-forties, in a uniform proclaiming her as *maître d'hôtel*, stepped forward and handed a bouquet to Jemima.

'Welcome to Routier, Miss Shore.' Roland Routier was taking Jemima's arm, leading her up the steps. 'So we're all set to make a good movie together?' She was steered through the reception committee without being introduced to anyone. 'I hope our book-keeper wasn't too much of a pain on the way down. All Dennis can talk is business. Very boring.'

To one side Jemima glimpsed the petulant toss of a dark head. It was one of the waitresses − without doubt the Italian girl Cherry had mentioned. Her eyes were indeed very dark and, right now, very stormy.

This was when Jemima's education in the niceties of entrails and appendages began. Although fervent with attentive phrases and wishes for her comfort while on his premises, and disdainful of his brother's drab concern with business, Routier lost little time in turning the conversation to his own business − or art − which was food. Jemima was shown the kitchens and listened to his ecstasies over his own brilliance in preparing tripe, brains, kidneys, and other delicacies. At the same time there was an echo at the back of her mind: had not Cherry reported similar outpourings from Georgie the cook, along with scorn for his employer's pretensions?

But she listened, nodded, and smiled. She was adept at deciding just when to draw people out and when to let them keep talking off their own bat. All the time she was sizing him up. Of course every restaurateur put on his own sort of act, and of course every one of them was as much an actor as a gourmet. So perhaps she was wrong in thinking that his coaxing voice and the sparkle in his eye were suggestive of something more than the mere need to get her to provide him with good publicity. Every woman customer was probably treated to the same insinuating manner.

As they strolled in the garden during the early evening, the sweep of his arm invited her to appreciate the scene. 'All this for a load of old tripe, eh?' He laughed a fraction too loudly, patting his wavy, dark brown hair. He had disposed of his tall chef's hat and was assuming a different, more proprietorial role.

'Tripe that gets three stars in the *Guide Michelin*,' she observed.

'Ah, that.' He tried to sound deprecating, but failed.

They followed a path along the water's edge. Ahead loomed a boat-house, more ornate than most of the riverside shacks Jemima had seen. This was almost like a miniature lodge, built of red and white brick, with an overhang supported by pillars between which bobbed a small but pricey motor-cruiser.

'How did you get into cooking?' asked Jemima.

'As a child I had a speech impediment. A therapist corrected it, but it took time. That and my love of water made me join the Navy.'

'I don't quite see —'

'As a steward. But I was more frequently beached than at sea. Always jumping ship for one reason or another. Usually the best one.' He slowed his pace. The brush of his hand on her arm might have been simply inviting her to share a joke. 'Women. Days gone by, Miss Shore.'

The path ended by a cluster of bushes and tall grasses, at the foot of an external staircase.

Routier nodded upwards. 'Champagne in the office, I think.'

'The office?'

'I get a lot more done up here than I'd ever manage in the main building. They think twice about coming over and disturbing me.'

It sounded like a hint, a reassurance.

Jemima felt in no need of reassurance along those lines. But she did raise an involuntary eyebrow when she saw the so-called office. Not many people would have been able to concentrate on accounts, recipes and menus in this riot of Chinoiserie, with its shaded lights and silken tassels. There were tent hangings with eastern love-scenes on the walls, and a large double divan suggested a love nest rather than a work room. As they entered, Routier must have thumbed a switch: quiet, suggestive music welled up into the room as if from the dreamy waters below.

He took a bottle of champagne from a refrigerator masquerading as an Oriental chest.

Jemima kept her distance. It was really getting too obvious. She began to realise that in a face-to-face conference with Roland Routier she might have been safer in high-necked chain mail and cast-iron greaves than in her grey trousers and white blouse.

Trying to keep the discussion on an even keel, she attempted: 'When you want to work out a new preparation of . . . well, let's say . . .'

'Offal is the food of love,' said Routier. 'The only genuinely aphrodisiac cuisine. That's why we keep five suites above the restaurant. Some couples just can't wait to get home.'

'Is this true?'

'Miss Shore, you have never made love after a plate of sweetbreads?'

'This brings a totally new social dimension to our programme,' she said sceptically. Guthrie would have admired her icy diction.

'Ah, yes. The recreational implications.' The champagne cork popped, and he reached for a glass from a nearby shelf. 'Ever heard of a man called Bartolomeo Scapolino?'

'The name doesn't immediately ring a bell.'

'He recorded over one hundred orgasms in twelve hours on a diet of sheep's brains and hydromel.' He handed her the glass and waited, smiling, for her reaction.

Jemima said: 'Let's just use our brains for this programme, shall we? Tomorrow we film the practical stuff. Intercut with a short interview and a few bits of straightforward explanation from you. Also we want to publish an accompanying booklet of recipes.'

'You really should test them first.' He drew closer. 'Make sure they have the properties I claim.'

A doorbell, just above the outer door, rang twice; three times.

Routier made a face. 'Who would have the . . .?' He marched across the room, nodding at a corner table with a silver dish and two plates on it. 'Help yourself to the caviar. It's almost offal.'

She heard him open the door and mutter something, then swear, and let out a snort of rage. His footsteps thumped down the steps outside. The door swung slowly shut of its own accord.

Jemima was glad of the respite. By the time he returned she would be even brisker and more impersonal than before. Evidently Routier was good at his profession − all the old camp and chat. She could predict that his camera personality would come over admirably, but he would need firm direction.

She must check with some tame dietician whether that stuff about sweetbreads being aphrodisiac was true.

Finishing her glass of champagne, Jemima nibbled a

caviar canapé and explored the walls in search of a window. She found one behind a tapestry depicting a convoluted nude, whose limbs writhed disconcertingly when the curtain was pulled a few inches aside.

Nobody moved below. There was no sound. Who was Routier talking to, if anyone? The river was calm, growing a darker shade of lead as the sun retreated. Lights had come on in the restaurant, and their reflections glinted across the placid surface.

Jemima had had enough of this. If her host had more important things to do than discuss the programme with her, she would go in search of better company.

As she made her way down the steps, a twig snapped and something shifted in the bushes.

'Mr Routier?'

There was no reply. She felt conscious of another presence, yet there was utter stillness now. Jemima stumbled on the bottom step, and steadied herself. Water plopped under the boat-house.

Impatiently she set off towards the glow-worm lights in the restaurant windows.

The staff were hurrying through their own dinner. In a far corner, Cherry sat leafing through a magazine. As Jemima went to join her, the *maître d'* jumped up from her chair and crossed the room.

'Good evening, Miss Shore. I hope everything –'

'Have you seen Mr Routier?'

'Mr Roland? I thought you were with him, Miss Shore.'

'I was, but he was called away. He's not in the kitchen?'

Betty shook her head. 'I haven't seen him anywhere.'

Jemima reached Cherry and sat down. 'Aren't you a bit early for dinner?'

'Guthrie's in a state. He wants me to bring your notes back. At the double.'

'What notes? Haven't had a chance to discuss anything properly. Waste of time. Opened a bottle of champagne, then vanished.'

Cherry watched young Colin head for the kitchen with the Italian girl. Cherry sighed. 'Georgie promised he'd make *Ris de veau Routier* specially for me, but I'm having to make do with the staff meal because he's gone off on the piss. There's some kind of aggro in the kitchen. But Gina says there's ox cheek and noodles. Should be all right. They're eating it themselves, anyway.'

'You're saying the cook's gone missing as well?'

It was ridiculous. Jemima sat back in her chair and studied the room disapprovingly. If this was how they coped with what could have been a big promotional asset, what were they like on ordinary days?

The Italian girl reappeared bearing a vast tray with a casserole and, beside it, a bowl of noodles. Her tempestuous face dripped barely controlled fury, as if the heat of the dishes had brought it out of her in a sweat.

'The bella Signorina Tee-Vee, she like helping also, please?'

Before Jemima could say that she preferred to wait and eat later, a plate was slammed down in front of her.

'Go on, Jemima,' urged Cherry: 'there's masses.'

Gina ladled one spoonful on to the plate. Then something snapped. The next second she was spooning out chunks of meat and hurling them at Jemima, dipping into the noodles and spreading them all over Jemima's lapels, her arm, her shoulder.

'Here, take it! Is good. Please, you have it all . . . you like? . . . and this . . .'

Jemima grabbed the girl's arm. It thrashed and struggled, powerful with rage. *'Lacha-me! Va fanculo!'*

Betty was rushing from the staff table.

'*Putana!*'

Betty clouted her about the head, and Gina went down, clawing at the tablecloth and pulling it off with a crashing and splintering of crockery and glass.

'A thousand apologies, Miss Shore. Colin – warm water and a towel. And fast.'

For once Jemima was almost at a loss for words. 'What on earth goes on around here?'

'Today is Wednesday,' Gina wailed. 'Is my day.'

'Unprecedented,' Betty apologised. 'Mr Roland picked her up in Rome, you see. Bound to lead to trouble, temperamental staff. No more Wednesdays for you, kid – whatever *they* may be,' she added hastily for Jemima's benefit.

Jemima sensed perfectly well what the Wednesdays might be. She thought of the boat-house, and of Roland Routier's leering face and his cosy arrangements there; and could almost have been sorry for Gina if she had not so recently been on the receiving end of Gina's rage.

Physically quelled but still seething, Gina leaned forward as if to spit on the liberal deposits of noodles. 'Tee-Vee jobs in de bot'ouse, huh? Uh-huh?'

Betty said: 'I'm afraid Mr Roland –'

'Plenty Tee-Vee with the champagne, huh?'

Jemima politely restrained Colin's frenzied dabbing with a sponge. And, frigidly polite, she said to Gina: 'I'm sorry I spoiled your afternoon with the boss. But everybody's honour is intacta. And now . . .' She moved away from the table with all the dignity she could muster, and it was enough: they all backed away. 'When you have finished your own meal, I'd like a bacon sandwich served in my suite, with a stick of celery. And a bottle of Hermitage blanc. Nicely chilled.'

'Yes, Miss. Gina will bring it to you.'

Gina twitched, but did not argue.

'And,' said Jemima, 'I'd like Mr Dennis to come and see me. It's important.'

She treated herself to a meditative bath, and changed into a dress bearing no lingering taint of cow's cheek and noodles. She had settled herself in an armchair, with the chill neck of the wine bottle in easy reach, when Dennis arrived, attired incongruously in a chef's apron, his sleeves pulled up by springy shirt bracelets.

In response to Jemima's stare of wonderment he snapped: 'Someone has to sort things out in the kitchen.'

'I take it they're both still missing? Do you suppose they're together?' When he could only shrug, she said: 'What do cooks do together, out on a spree? Discuss menus? Go fishing – or hunt the truffle and win trackers' badges? Do they devise new *marinades*?'

Dennis tugged at his right sleeve like a man rolling it up before taking a punch at someone. 'Betty saw George steal two bottles of vodka from the cocktail bar.'

Jemima mused that, however unrewarding she might be as company for a clumsy lecher, Roland Routier would hardly have walked out on her just in search of a drink. He had, after all, just opened a bottle of vintage champagne.

'I tell you,' Dennis was ranting on, 'I'm choked with it all. Chockablock. And now, if you'll excuse me, I'd better go and see what the hell is going on downstairs.'

'One minute, Mr Jones.' Jemima, too, was choked and chocka. 'You've got a contract for a nice fat facility fee. And I've got a script to prepare, and you lot are supposed to go along with it. So just what sort of deal do you call *this*?'

Those muscular hands clenched, slackened, and clenched again. He had no intention of chucking Jemima up in the air, but she could tell he would gladly have done so to somebody else. Words came grinding out.

'I'll tell you what I call the whole thing, Miss Shore. If you really want to know – really want the juicy story – our dear Roland leads the life of Riley. Talk of keeping up with the Joneses: just you try and keep up the pace of the Routier. Cook Georgie goes crazy drunk every three months, and who has to pick up the pieces? Me, like always. It isn't my name above the door – it's just under everybody else's feet. Madame's got her shops, and Mister bloody Roland's got everything.'

The phone rang. A woman's voice asked for Mr Jones. Jemima jabbed the receiver at him.

In a pathetically posh voice Dennis said: 'Mr Dennis here.' Then the accent collapsed. 'No, Monica. I told you he was with that TV lot. Jemima Shore, yes. Well, no: I think they were at the boat-house, but Miss Shore's right here now. All right, all right. Maybe you'd best have a word with her.'

Jemima agreed that it was indeed best for the two of them to have a word. Dennis's face clouded as he heard her make the appointment for an immediate visit and then clatter the phone down.

'I thought you had a script to prepare,' he said sourly.

'First I have to find my star.'

'You think you'll find him at home?'

She was glad to be out of the building. A moment of fresh air, and then there was the comfort and familiarity of her car. She flicked the radio on, and found herself in the middle of the catalogue aria from Mozart's *Don Giovanni*. She thought ruefully of Routier and was glad not to have been added to his own private catalogue.

As she swung on to the drive and headed for the gates, something white swayed in her headlights, like a sheet of paper trapped by a cross-current. Only it wasn't a sheet of paper, but a chef's hat. Below it, a figure clothed in white swayed to one side and then stumbled out of the glare, coming to rest against the wall of the old stable block. Light glinted from the vodka bottle which Georgie was tipping up towards his mouth. Jemima flung open the door and advanced on him. Blearily he tried to wave her away.

'Chef, it's me. Jemima Shore. Cherry's friend. You promised her –'

'I do not want. Not want to be in your bloody film.'

'Have you any idea where Mr Routier –'

'Let the bastard do it himself.' The empty bottle shattered on the ground. 'He do it himself, yes? Let us see him, let us . . .' Georgie's fat shape quivered and went wobbling off into a clump of trees.

Jemima took a few steps in pursuit. A trailing branch slashed at her legs. The shadows under the trees did not frighten her, but she did not fancy the effect they would have on her dress – or on her face. Whatever drunken misery possessed Georgie, there was precious little she could do about it tonight. Even as an object lesson in what happened to people who cooked too much offal, he was not in the best mood to be interviewed.

She went back to the car and proceeded towards the Routier house, following the slightly bossy but accurate instructions which Roland's wife had given her over the phone.

Monica Routier bore the trophies of a successful business career in the shape of large rings, a heavily jewelled bracelet, and a pendant which must represent a sizeable chunk of the profits over the years. Her study was effectively divided in two: at one end stood an uncluttered desk and filing cabinets, overlooked by a pinboard stuck with reminders; at the other were comfortable armchairs and a coffee table, and an array of pot plants flanking a cosily flickering imitation log fire. Above the fire, dominating the room, was a painting of a woman seated by a window whose shutter had been drawn back to frame a sunlit harbour beyond.

'I always settle myself in here when I'm alone,' said Monica. 'I can work, or read, or watch television if I'm in the mood. I've seen your programme, but I've got to be honest, I can't say I watch it regularly.'

'If I had that painting I'm not sure I would, either,' said Jemima lightly.

'That's my treasure.'

So it should be. Jemima contrasted the atmosphere in this room with that in what purported to be the husband's study.

Her hostess was pouring coffee. As she handed Jemima a cup she said abruptly: 'Why do you want to film at Routier? Nothing unsavoury to dig up there, my dear. The kitchen's spotless and we serve fresh food.'

'I'm sure you do.'

'Pricey, I grant you. But it's cheap for the best offal cuisine in the world. I mean, where else would you find roast lambs' intestines and sour snout soup under the same roof?'

'That's what my film's about.'

'Well, if you want to go into it properly, you've picked the right man.'

'Except that we've lost him.'

'Oh, dear. Taken one of his turns, has he?' Monica sipped her coffee, unperturbed. 'He'll be back. Paris, New York, Brighton, you name it – he's been there and back.' She gazed up with indefinable melancholy at the painting. 'Look at that, dear. That man painted the most sensual women in France; but he always came back. His wife was waiting. Like me. We have a flat in Nice, four doors down from the house where he used to live. I've got a room with that beach view, too, just the same, so it could be my own portrait, really.'

Jemima wondered how to put a stop to this maudlin flow. 'So wherever Mr Routier's nipped off to this time, you think he'll –'

'I've been worrying about him lately. A lot. Fifty-four, you know, and still carrying on like he's Errol Flynn. Last year he had some trouble with his teeth. I was so pleased. Our dentist wanted to pull them out and I thought, now that'll slow him down – I mean, with false teeth, dear.'

'Yes,' said Jemima helplessly.

'But he went into the clinic and came out with them all capped. Six thousand pounds. Now he's worse.' Monica's gaze swung unexpectedly towards Jemima. 'I suppose he made a pass at you, dear?'

'I . . . we were talking business . . .'

'When's that ever stopped him?'

'Well, I did think he might have been working up to something, but really it was only a harmless –'

'Champagne?'

'Yes.'

'And caviar.' Monica's lips puckered knowingly. 'Oh, he tries them all. And scores quite a lot. My friends, titled customers, the lot. But you should have seen him when he was a young man.'

Jemima put her head back against the chair. A faint, lingering scent drifted into her consciousness for a moment, and she turned her head. It was puzzling, somehow reminiscent – but of what?

Resolutely she said: 'Now, do tell me more about the organisation. About Georgie, for a start.'

She had chosen the right name to prompt a diversion. Monica wanted to make it clear that she had the greatest admiration for Georgie. They all had. He was a wonderful, creative cook. Nobody could deny that. But he was temperamental, there was no getting away from it. And not, in the long run, up to Roly's standard. Roly was the one with the real flair. He had been born to the game. As she went on, it was clear that in spite of her jealousies and suspicions there was nobody else in the world for her but Roland Routier.

Jemima took away with her a more substantial batch of notes than she had succeeded in getting from the elusive Routier himself. Fired, as so often before, by the urge to shape everything up in the right order for the basic script, she went to bed early, propped herself up against the pillows in her bedroom, and set to work. It was so much easier to work at a time like this, in the stillness, uninterrupted.

Uninterrupted . . . until there came a light tapping at the door of the sitting room, faint but more and more insistent.

Jemima slipped into her dressing-gown and padded out of the bedroom. 'Who is it?'

'Open. You please open.'

Outside the door stood Georgie. He had drunk himself sober but still looked very much the worse for wear. His chef's hat was on straight, but was badly smeared with dirt. A knife and a wooden spoon were stuck into the cord of his apron. He was leaning heavily on a trolley, which began to roll forward as soon as Jemima opened the door.

'*Brioche de foie de canard truffée,*' he intoned reverently. '*Fromage de tête au porto.*' With a dramatic gesture he took the knife from his apron and flicked back the cloth from a dish. 'I promise Miss Cherry, I make her something special, now she is not here but they tell me she has gone to London, so I ask you please –'

'Just a minute, now. I'm not sure I'm hungry, not after all that's been going on.'

Georgie swayed, squinted at one of the silver serving dishes, and made a sudden lunge at it with the knife. On its tip he lifted a steaming morsel of meat.

'You try this.'

She thought it safest to obey; but her 'Mmm' was quite spontaneous.

'Is good?' Georgie's podgy, glistening face pleaded for her approval.

Good it was. She nodded enthusiastically.

'I lose my temper, you understand,' he said. 'But it is over. I work in your film.'

'Have you seen Mr Routier?' she challenged him.

'Oh, that's OK. Roly an' me, we are buddies, you know. He used to me by now.'

'Where *is* he?'

'Home with his Monique.' Georgie frowned in an effort to recollect. 'I hope so.'

'Routier has not been home. No one has seen him since he left me. In the boat-house.'

'No one?' Georgie's eyes were coming into reluctant focus. He looked genuinely stunned.

'No.'

Georgie gulped. 'Come, please. I know where he is.'

'You do?'

'We . . . we have a fight. I hit him.'

Letting out a little sob, he touched her arm. Apprehensively Jemima went out with him into the night. As they paced across the grass, damp with the night dew, he began to chatter compulsively.

'I say to him, they are *my recettes*, so this time I do the Tee-Vee. And this one Dennis, the weight lifter, he is the nothing, you understand. And Roly say sure, I am to be the assistant. The *assistant*! I tell you, Miss Shore,

Routier he take the *Medaille d'Or de la Société de Paris* with *my* marrow dumpling *recette*. He win everything for Routier. But tomorrow it is I, I am the one who show my cow-heel pie because it is mine and that is it.'

'I had no idea you actually created so many dishes.'

'So many? All. *I* am the chef. Do you not understand?'

They had reached the boat-house. Jemima put a hand on the railing and looked up the steps.

'It was you who rang the doorbell?' she asked. When the distorted shadow of his lolling head nodded, she said: 'All right. So Mr Routier opens the door to you and comes out. Then what?'

'He tells me is busy, tells me keep my voice down. And comes down here. And I grab him, and he say all right, I will do the Tee-Vee. But because I know him, I say I talk with Miss Shore and I get her signature and I have contract, too. No, no, do me a favour, not now, Jo-Jo, that is what he say. I am going to make love to her, he say.'

'Does he?' said Jemima dryly.

'At his tricks again. So I hit him. I push him this way, over here,' moaned Georgie, 'and I hit him.'

He waved a wretched hand towards the planking of the jetty which ran deep under the boat-house.

Even in that uncertain gloom Jemima was sure there was nobody there. She stooped to see better; and at the same time there was the rustle and crunch of footsteps. The beam of a torch stabbed at them, and behind it she could just make out a dark figure carrying what appeared to be an iron bar.

'What are *you* doing out here?' It was the voice of Dennis Jones.

'We think . . . Georgie thinks . . . your brother may have . . . had an accident.'

The torchlight explored the empty interior of the mooring space, then swung out across the water. Something heaved and bumped across the bank. A tangle of ropes snared by a stanchion twisted around each other like the dripping tresses of some mythical sea creature.

'There!' wailed Georgie.

'Hold on to me.' Jemima edged down the steep side of the bank, with Dennis holding one arm and leaning out to prod the bar into the ropes and weed.

A body turned over slowly, like a sleepy porpoise. The light gleamed on a forehead, and rippled up and over. There was no chef's hat on Roland Routier's head now. Nor was there any hair: only a faint trail of green slime crossed his pale, bald head.

'It's Roly,' groaned Dennis. He floundered waist-deep into the water, freeing his brother from the ropes which had held him against the stanchion. 'He wore a wig.'

Roland Routier wore it no longer. Not that he needed to be proud or secretive about anything any longer. He was dead.

In the immediate responsibility of notifying the police, breaking the news to the staff first thing in the morning, and preparing to make a statement to the local inspector while a forensic expert worked his way along the boat-house wall and the jetty, Jemima forgot just one thing. Guthrie Carlyle and the camera team were due to set out early from London in order to get here and start shooting. When she remembered, it was too late to stop them. The police photographer was none too pleased to have other cameramen trampling through the building and rigging up lights on the terrace. But Guthrie proceeded to set up the whole operation as if nothing had happened which could not be smoothly incorporated into the programme.

Inspector Norries watched a frogman surfacing a few yards out in the river, and sniffed – not at the frogman but at the all-pervading smell.

'Creosote,' he grunted. 'Hopeless stuff. Kills every trace of everything.'

'Skip, I've found it!' The frogman flapped ashore and held out what looked like a bedraggled scalp. It was Routier's wig.

Any examination of this, for all the good it would do, was cut short by a piercing shriek from across the lawn. Someone in the restaurant was screaming with all the force of a powerful pair of lungs – screaming out through the open window at the near end of the terrace. The inspector eyed Jemima, and together they ran across the grass.

In the dining room an unlovely scrimmage was going on. Betty, the *maître d'*, was lying crumpled in a chair while a policewoman sought to restrain a spitting, threshing, screeching Gina.

'*Lacha-me . . . porca! . . .* ayee . . .!'

'Dalton, what's this?' demanded Norries.

'The Eyetalian lady, sir –'

'She tried to lamp me with the champagne bucket.' Betty struggled upright.

'She call me bloody whore.'

'You *are* a bloody whore.'

'Ladies, ladies!'

'An' she keel him.' Gina tugged an arm free and stabbed an accusing finger at Betty. '*E vero*. She keel him because she hate me, because she jealous old *gatto*. I tell Miss Tee-Vee. I know it . . .'

'One thing I do know,' said Norries with admirable calm, 'is that statements make more sense if you tackle them one at a time.'

The dining room was cleared. It looked very wide

and empty in the morning sunlight.

Inspector Norries began with Betty, who proudly stated her case and gave evidence without mincing her words. Yes, she had been Routier's mistress. For all of sixteen years. Gina had been nothing but his tart, like a French girl before her and a Paddy before that. She had been his Wednesday girl, while some of the others — including even the cleaning woman — shared his favours whenever it suited him.

'That's how he was,' said Betty, with no apparent sign of resentment.

'Did he always take you to the boat-house?'

'When he'd got time to spare. Other times it was in the office behind reception. Or across the pantry table. Anywhere he liked.'

It was clear that the inspector, a family man himself, did not approve of this. But with unruffled courtesy he asked: 'Now, how do you think Mrs Routier coped with .. with all this going on?'

'Very nicely, thank you.' The first trace of bitterness crept into Betty's tone. 'She had him to herself at home. They had their holidays together in the south of France. She should worry.'

'Did you ever go to their flat there?'

'What, me? Never. Nor to her shops. And she never came here. Mr Roland made that rule soon after he started the restaurant. All the decorations and flowers she bought were delivered. I was Mr Roland's woman in charge here. Me and nobody else.'

At last she broke down and began to cry.

Together the inspector and Jemima sifted through the facts and speculations. He had taken her into his confidence from the start, without any fuss and without openly acknowledging that he knew her to be the widely publicised Jemima Shore, Investigator. His steady confidence was attractive and reassuring. Between them they could sort this out ... she hoped.

It was crudely obvious that Routier had run part of his premises as a personal bordello; yet he had in many ways been a model employer. Most of them liked him, even at his worst; and some of them doted on him.

'Except for Dennis,' said Inspector Norries. 'He doesn't give me the impression of being an adoring brother.'

'Nor me,' Jemima agreed. 'He was the odd job man, and I think he hated it.'

'If that chef gets done for manslaughter, Dennis takes over the restaurant.'

Jemima brooded over this. 'Even if Georgie bashed Routier and then pushed him in, he surely wouldn't have drifted like that. I mean ... I mean, do *you* mean that Dennis could have thrown him into the river?'

'Olympic weight-lifter,' said Norries significantly.

'He was shaken when we found the body. He wasn't faking that.'

The moment she said it, she realised that Dennis could have been shaken because the corpse had been caught up by a stanchion instead of floating away as he had planned.

In the distance there resounded a familiar command. The team was beginning to shoot scenes in the kitchen, and clamorous voices were demanding silence. Inspector Norries grunted condemnation of yet another aspect of this case. For a moment Jemima wondered if he was going to ask her to clear her people off the premises; but he made no comment, and the unit went ahead. Colin was an unimpressive substitute for the volatile – but now prostrate – Georgie. Jemima spent a few unrewarding minutes watching him in full spate, from which the only pleasure she derived was the sight of Guthrie's stricken expression as Colin squeaked rapturously about blanched tripe and 'piggie's trotters', which he waggled in a sickly bye-bye as he snuggled them down into the marmite and vegetables. She was not unwilling to be drawn away by Inspector Norries just when the unit's gaffer announced that there was no way his lads were going to eat a meal here, not after seeing what was kept in the fridge.

'I've fixed an interview with Mrs Routier,' said Norries in an undertone. 'She seems quite happy at the idea of you sitting in. Sounded quite curious about you.'

'I can guess why,' said Jemima.

From his faint smile she realised that he, too, could guess why; and she felt a stir of anger against that insufferable, randy, prancing man – that dead man who'd so savagely been given his come-uppance, she reminded herself before she grew too censorious.

Seated in Monica Routier's den before her desk, Jemima regretted not being in a position to contemplate that radiant painting. It would have been more comforting than the drawn features of the woman waiting for the interrogation to begin.

Behind Monica's head, two slips of theatre ticket still dangled from the pinboard. Jemima had idly noticed them last night. Now her gaze was dragged compulsively back to them.

Gently Norries said: 'Mrs Routier, could you tell me about your movements yesterday afternoon?'

'Certainly. I left the England's Lane shop at four o'clock and drove to Grove Farm Garden Centre. Got there at four-forty.' She was crisp and concise. 'I checked that because I was kept waiting for seven minutes. I ordered flowers and plants, and left at five-fifteen. That gave me time to catch Jennings the greengrocer and be home by six.'

'And after that?'

'I waited for Roly. As I always did.' She lowered her eyes. 'I phoned the restaurant twice, but they hadn't a clue. Then Miss Shore came. By the way, I've instructed Dennis that the filming must go on. I see it as a tribute to Roly.'

'I'm sure it will be.' Jemima got up, paused – something was nagging at her, something on the edge of awareness – and then made for the door. 'I think I'd better get back and see what they're up to.'

What they were up to was little enough. The unit had broken for an early lunch in the pub down the road; Guthrie thought the whole job was a bummer and wanted to call a wrap; and Cherry, looking soggy-eyed from lack of sleep, showed signs of agreeing with him. Before Jemima could summon them all back for a salutary lecture on professional responsibility, she was trapped by Georgie.

If Cherry's eyes were soggy, Georgie's were a pink-tinted fenland. 'Miss Shore, you get me good lawyers, yes? Many of them, please. And I confess I kill Roly. I think I kill him when I was mad, you know.'

Carefully Jemima said: 'You told me you pushed him, and hit him. You saw him on the boards of the jetty?'

'That is it. I am killer.'

'The police are still trying to establish exactly where he fell.'

'I hit him so hard, maybe I hit him over.'

Jemima tried her best dictatorial voice. 'You didn't kill him, Georgie. That I'll bet on. And you are going to be the star of my programme, just the way you wanted it.' She escaped what might have been a loving hug, and veered away. 'Now I want a word with Gina.'

Gina, as might have been predicted, was not interested in a word. A hundred words, yes; and at a staggeringly high decibel count. But out of the tirade Jemima learned what she had half guessed and now knew in full. She let it assemble itself as she went out towards the boat-house, jarred by the recollection of previous walks in that direction – to the boat-house with Routier, back in the twilight, and then over that same route to find the corpse. Smell of the grass, of the flower-beds, of that pungent creosote whose smell you carried round in your nostrils for hours . . .

Creosote.

She stopped; then moved more slowly towards the flight of steps to the top floor of the boat-house. She was reminded of the rustling of the tall grass, and now in daylight saw where a swathe had been trampled through them. Someone had been here. And not just last night, by the look of it: the patch in the middle had been thoroughly flattened, as if by someone regularly sunbathing.

'Find any clues, duckie?'

She started. Dennis was watching her from the shade of the garden wall.

'Enough,' she said.

In the upstairs room of the boat-house, with its garish decorations looking bedraggled and of no significance now, she joined Inspector Norries and Monica Routier.

Monica was inspecting the place with mounting disgust. 'I've never been here before. Questionable taste, wouldn't you say, dear?' She stared accusingly at Jemima. 'And you let him bring you up here?'

'You never know what you're letting yourself in for,' said Jemima levelly, 'until it's there in front of you. So let's talk about this room.'

'Yes, do let's.'

'And,' said Jemima, 'about the four people involved in the murder of Roland Routier.'

'Four? Seems everybody's getting on to her telly show. Do you mind, inspector?'

'Miss Shore has been very helpful.' Norries was giving nothing away, but Jemima sensed that he was as tense and watchful as she was.

'Whoopee for her.'

Jemima felt the pulse of her heart quickening. 'Your husband had his day off on Sunday and a half-day on Wednesday. His routine was to finish the lunchtime service and then bring his bit of stuff back here for a siesta, returning home to you at six. This week was different, though. Yesterday he cancelled his afternoon assignation with his Wednesday girl because it was your wedding anniversary. Twenty years. Correct, Mrs Routier?'

'I don't see what that –'

'You didn't mention it to me last night. But you had tickets' – she pointed to the slips on the corner of the board – 'for Covent Garden. *Don Giovanni*. I heard part of the live relay on Radio 3.'

'Is it relevant?'

'Routier told Gina you'd made him promise not to make love to her on your big day.'

'Rubbish. What he does here is here.'

'I've just been talking to Gina. She told me.'

'He would never have talked about personal things like that. Never.'

'You didn't trust him,' said Jemima inexorably. 'Which is why you came straight here from the garden centre and hid in the bushes. Not so much to pry – though you'd done that before – but to prove to yourself that on this special occasion he was really going to keep his promise. And so it would have been if I hadn't appeared on the scene. Perhaps he'd still be alive if he hadn't brought me here.'

Monica looked at her; at Inspector Norries; and in

silent prayer at her beloved painting. In spite of what she knew – what she must assuredly know – did she still expect Roland miraculously to return, and be the Roland she had known and loved so long ago?

'You were watching,' said Jemima. 'And all at once Georgie appears, drunk and doddering across the grass, ringing the doorbell. And when Routier comes down, Georgie goes for him and shoves him into the mooring bay –'

'That's my Georgie,' said Monica dully.

'You saw Georgie knock your husband out and go blundering off. Then you went over to the jetty, and after you'd disposed of your husband you leaned back against the wall to recover.'

'You couldn't possibly –'

'Smudging creosote on your coat,' said Jemima, 'which I could still smell in your study when I got there. I imagine you threw your coat over the chair while you sat down and got your breath back – was that it?'

Monica was numb, motionless.

'It was Georgie who knocked Routier out,' said Jemima, 'but it was you who coldly rolled him into the river.'

'Coldly?' There was a catch in her voice, an instinctive crackle of protest.

'You drowned him.'

Inspector Norries was sitting almost as still as Monica. His muscles and the set of his mouth relaxed only when she said: 'I was going to intervene. Truly I was. But I heard what he was boasting about. What he fancied doing to you. Such vile, disgusting stuff. And then he was sneering about me and about our anniversary. He called me . . .' For a moment she bent in on herself and could not speak. Then she forced herself to continue. 'I thought that deep down, really, he loved me. In his own way. Somehow. But after what I heard . . . oh, our life together was never anything but make-believe.' She took one last imploring glance at the painting, then turned to the inspector. 'I'm glad I went to the boat-house. And I'm glad there's no pretending any more.'

The rest of the day and the next day were a nightmare which Jemima would have been glad to write off. But she could hardly lecture her crew on professional responsibility and then chicken out herself. They went on with the filming, put Georgie in the star place he had coveted, and then had to scatter as he went into a tantrum after fluffing his lines and laid about him with a knife too large and sharp for comfort. One queasy girl complained of Jemima's callousness in ordering them to film fried brains so soon after the master chef had had his head bashed in. It was a relief to be packing up at last, getting ready to quit that luxurious yet unwelcoming suite which the dead Roland Routier had put at Jemima's disposal.

'Guthrie was right,' she admitted. 'Volatile stuff, all that cooking of innards. Not for people of cool temperament. Guthrie's heart wasn't in it.'

'On the subject of hearts' – Cherry was having a last snack from something which Georgie had provided on a tray – 'this is sensational.'

The end of an era, thought Jemima. Routier had been the driving force behind this place, and she could not envisage Dennis or anyone else carrying it on. Certainly not the widow. Norries, bleak yet sympathetic, had prophesied that she would be treated tolerantly – she had already served a twenty-year sentence of humiliation – but there was no way, now or later, that she could keep things going here, even if she had wanted to.

Cherry said, at the door: 'I wonder what would have

happened if you and Routier the Raving Rake hadn't been interrupted?'

'Let's say I was lucky. Saved by the bell.' Jemima picked up her case; Cherry swung her typewriter in that casual way which had threatened many a male kneecap. 'Let's go. Early start tomorrow. We've got a slot to fill, to make up for this one. Guthrie's fixing us up with a Welsh seaweed factory.'

# Promising Death

Sunday, Jemima always reckoned, was a dull day. Perhaps this feeling was a hangover from her time at her convent boarding school. Most of the girls there were weekly boarders, and so went home for the weekend, but Jemima could never do that after her first year. She had gone to Churne as a day girl when her parents had been stationed there, but her father had been in the Army, and her parents were subsequently stationed all over the world. And then, just before she went up to Cambridge, they were killed in a car crash in Hong Kong. So, throughout her later school years, apart from a couple of weekends a term with an elderly aunt or a school friend at home, Sundays were spent at school. Jemima realised, looking back, that this enforced solitude had developed her love of reading, and the independence and self-reliance which was now so useful, but it had been hard at the time. Now that Sundays were hers to arrange as she liked, Jemima liked company. Her pre-lunch Sunday drinks were an institution amongst her friends.

This particular Sunday, Cherry was there. She had just finished one of her disastrous love affairs, and needed cheering up, so Jemima had asked her along – reckoning that if Cherry helped serve the drinks, she had an excuse to meet all Jemima's guests. Unfortunately, this benign plan was going awry: Cherry had been buttonholed by Mr Troyne, an elderly academic of intense earnestness. He was expounding something at great length – probably his special subjects of bibliography and holography, about which Jemima had already had his lecture. Jemima wondered what on earth had possessed her old publishing friend Miles to bring the man along: he was stunningly boring.

That description also looked like applying to the latest companion of her old university friend Vee Brewer, who was trying to down as much drink as he could in the shortest possible time. Jemima hoped it might be nerves, but she had her doubts.

Vee had been at the same college as Jemima. They had both read English Literature, and Vee now edited the highly influential (but small circulation) literary magazine *Critique*. Sometimes, Jemima felt, Vee had never really left the 'sixties. She was still a hippy at heart, and had a penchant for lost causes and lame-dog lovers, who all too often worked out their inadequacies by doing her violence. Her current lover was no exception. A member of the East End underworld, Billy Standen had briefly been the darling of the literary scene when his first novel had come out a few years previously. It had appeared shortly after his release from prison for attempted murder, an emotional diatribe against the oppression of prison life. Now, he was writing a series of articles for *New Society* about the Arts in British prisons. Several of Jemima's programmes had discussed prison conditions, and she was well aware that Vee was trying to get Billy onto a show.

Jemima rather prided herself on choosing people for her parties. But this time, her carefully considered mix did not seem to be gelling. Billy had driven most people from the kitchen with his drunken tirades against the middle classes (although he was only too keen to drink their booze, she noted). Then there was Mr Troyne. Jemima was just about to go and rescue Cherry from him, when the doorbell rang. She went to it herself.

'Sweets to the sweet,' purred Jamie Grand, as he stood in her doorway holding out an enormous bouquet of white roses. 'I hope you don't mind,' he said, 'but I've brought a young friend with me.' Standing behind Jamie –a literary critic friend – was a very English-looking man with fair hair and clear blue eyes.

'Nick!' exclaimed Jemima, with pleasure. They embraced. Obviously pleased with himself, Jamie pretended to look surprised.

'Oh, you've met?' he murmured innocently.

He had hardly changed at all, Jemima thought. She hoped she still looked as young as *he* did all these years after their university days. Nick had been another of Jemima's contemporaries at Cambridge, and they had a brief but passionate affair during her first summer up. But they had drifted apart in the hectic pace of university life, and she had not seen him since. He had got a First, she knew, and had become a high-flyer in the Foreign Office, but she had heard nothing more until his first novel had been published recently. *The Long Death of a Hill* had been greeted with great acclaim, and Nick was now one of London's young literary lions. A genuinely shy, retiring person, Nick was still rather bewildered by his meteoric success, and the constant stream of invitations to literary parties. And now, Jemima thought, one could apply that tag to *her* party, with Vee, Billy, Jamie – and now Nick.

Nick's initial appearance of languid aloofness, and his upper-class public-school accent, immediately antagonised Billy, who was well on his way, by this time, to becoming belligerently drunk. Billy was further riled by the attention that Vee was showing Nick. She was part of a coterie sitting round Nick at the kitchen table.

'It is so wonderful to be excited by new talent,' she purred.

'I was just lucky to be reviewed in a week when everything was pretty feeble,' Nick shrugged in a self-deprecating manner.

This was more than Billy could bear: his latest book had been reviewed in the same week, and had scarcely raised a murmur. Slamming the bottle he was clutching hard down onto the table, he snarled at Nick. 'I don't come to parties to have the piss taken out of my books!'

Nick blinked. He had no idea what Billy was angry about.

Vee tried, ineffectively, to calm down Billy, who was working himself up into a terrible rage. 'He called it "feeble". I've never been feeble in my life, pal! "Feeble" is not what people call me. Not if they want to walk home in one piece.'

The fracas attracted Jemima's attention. She had been chatting to Jamie in the sitting room. It really was too much, she thought, as she strode through the archway between the sitting room and the kitchen. One could stand only so much bad behaviour from one's friends. Billy had gone too far.

'Billy,' she admonished in her most school-teacherly tone. He seemed to suddenly realise the embarrassment he was causing Vee, and turned to leave. He brushed past Jemima, but then stopped, turned and pointed his finger at Nick. 'I'll see you again, pal!'

Vee apologised for Billy's behaviour and bustled out after him.

A wave of relief was audible throughout the party. Nick glanced up at Jemima. 'Vicious, this literary world, isn't it,' he muttered, with diffident irony. There was obviously more to this man than Jemima could remember. She refilled his glass, which he had been clutching rather nervously throughout Billy's outburst, and sat down next to him, in the place vacated by Vee.

Jemima had not known, at Cambridge, that he had wanted to write. Jokingly, she rebuked him for not having let her read his work. She could look at the book he had just finished, he offered.

Jamie was delighted at reintroducing the old flames, and at the obvious rapport that there still was between them. Patting Nick on the shoulder, he leant down and asked, teasingly, 'The question is, though, can you pull off the trick again? Or are you just a bungalow writer?'

'Bungalow writer?' chorused Nick and Jemima.

'One story!' Jamie smiled.

Well, thought Jemima, she would find out from this new book. His first novel had greatly impressed her. Trust old Jamie to find the latest talent and bring it to meet her.

The rest of the drinks party passed off smoothly. The bother at the beginning was soon forgotten, and it was – all in all – another Jemima Shore success. Gradually, people began to drift off, but before Nick left to return to his writing, he arranged to take Jemima out to dinner. Jemima's old interest in Nick was beginning to revive.

The news of his death was therefore a greater shock than it might have been. Nick had been shot in the back, on his Kentish Town doorstep, when he returned from Jemima's party. He had been opening the street door to the stairs to his pokey flat above a Bulgarian craft shop called 'Katerina'. Her genuine shock was changed to a more positive interest when Jamie rang up demanding to see her. He wanted to talk about Nick's death. He was so insistent that she suspected there must be a puzzle somewhere for her to solve.

Calling her contacts at the Met., Jemima discovered that the police were convinced the death was a case of mistaken identity. It seemed that Nick had been mistaken for a Bulgarian agent of some sort and had been 'eliminated'.

This official explanation however, did not convince Jamie. When they met at a wine bar, he tried to tease Jemima into coming up with some other theories. Jemima toyed with her glass of Sancerre that Jamie had so thoughtfully bought, knowing it to be one of her favourites.

'Well,' she said, eventually, not sounding very convinced, 'there's Vee Brewer's bit of literary rough trade.'

'Billy?'

'Yes, but Vee gives him an alibi for the time of the shooting. I can always double check though.'

Jamie shook his head and bemoaned Nick's death, not just for the loss of a human being but as a tragic waste of talent. He had been very promising.

'Whom the gods wish to destroy, they first call promising,' misquoted Jemima.

'Well, the gods certainly did a thorough job on Nick Beckleigh,' Jamie added.

Turning over various ideas in her head, Jemima wondered whether Nick had got on the wrong side of any foreign authority whilst in the Foreign Office. Jamie pointed out that, if so, they had taken their time to wreak retribution, because he had left it over four years ago. Nor had there been anything in *The Long Death of a Hill* to antagonise anyone.

'What about the second book?' asked Jemima.

They were coming, Jemima sensed, to the point of

the meeting. Jamie leant forward in the large, comfortable sofa and said, confidingly, 'That's the disturbing thing, Jemima – there is no second book.'

'But he was going to show it to me.'

'I know, but there's no sign of the manuscript.'

Perplexed, Jemima asked who had searched for it. That, Jamie explained, appeared to be the problem. Nick's wife – or rather about-to-be ex-wife, since the divorce papers would have been through in another fortnight – had been nothing but a hindrance to his writing, but she was now his literary executor. Mrs Beckleigh claimed she had searched, but could find no manuscript.

'I wish somebody could find out,' Jamie said, obviously trying to sound nonchalant, 'whether the manuscript exists.'

Jemima looked at Jamie, her Investigator's nose already twitching. There was no need for him to be so roundabout in his approach.

'That casual tone won't work,' she teased. 'I always know just what you mean when you use it.'

'Good. I knew you'd have a go!' Jamie now relaxed his bulk back into the sofa's soft cushions.

The first call on her quest for the missing manuscript and the real reason for Nick Beckleigh's death, Jemima decided, would be Vee Brewer.

Vee Brewer's flat reflected her personality. Afghan rugs covered those walls which did not have book cases against them, and strange, violent metal sculptures stood by the window of the living room, where the only seats were large, brightly coloured floor cushions. Books were piled up all over the place – sometimes doing duty as small tables.

A large expresso machine and two chipped mugs were

perched on one of those piles. Reaching for her mug of coffee Jemima tried to avoid looking her friend directly in the face, which despite great attempts with make-up, could not conceal the blueish marks of a black eye. She was not convinced by Vee's protests that Billy was really very gentle, but his alibi for the time of Nick's murder was confirmed. They had gone straight back home after Jemima's party, and made love. Following that, Vee had sat up and read in bed whilst Billy slept next to her. Vee agreed, however, that Billy was extremely jealous of Nick's critical success.

'How well did you know Nick?' asked Jemima, trying to get off the subject of Billy's problems, about which, she knew, Vee could spend hours talking.

'I only met him when his book came out. It was just so good that I had to get to know him.'

'Did he talk to you about his writing?'

Vee nodded, 'Yes, he did. He also told me how he wrote.' She was warming to the conversation. 'I do think it interesting and revealing how people do the actual mechanics of writing. Don't you? He always wrote in long-hand, in 2B pencil, and in ruled school exercise books.'

'But what about the subject matter of his second book?'

'He was very secretive about that. . . .' She paused, but then added proudly, 'It was quite a job just getting the title out of him.'

'What was it?' Jemima asked impatiently.

'*The Father-in-Law's Tale*,' Vee replied, going on immediately to berate Nick's wife for being totally un-sympathetic and lacking in understanding. Jemima noted, with wry amusement, that Vee had the grace to touch her eye involuntarily as she spoke.

*

Nick's widow, Lottie Beckleigh, was not too keen to meet Jemima at the Kentish Town flat. Jemima arrived first, and waited outside the shabby shop. After a couple of minutes, an attractive woman, expensively dressed and with an expensive accent, came up to her.

'Miss Shore,' she said (having a well-known face was useful sometimes – no need for rolled newspapers or carnations). 'I am only doing this, Miss Shore,' she continued, as she unlocked the door to the stairs which led up to the flat above, 'because my father said I should. He doesn't like muck-raking journalists – but he doesn't like suspicion either.'

'Absolutely right.'

'I've got nothing to hide.'

'Fine,' asserted Jemima. She wasn't so sure of that, but Vee had been absolutely right on one thing. Mrs Lottie Beckleigh was surprisingly unhelpful.

'Nick's agent asked me to look through all this rubbish.' Lottie waved her hand dismissively at the immaculately tidy but spartan flat. It was a complete contrast to Vee's bohemian home, verging on being disturbingly precise. The bare walls were covered by tall filing cabinets, and there wasn't a single personal photo or memento on display.

'I didn't find the manuscript you asked about. But if you want to double check, be my guest.'

Jemima nodded her thanks, and methodically began to examine the filing cabinets. As she worked through them, Lottie watched her, talking contemptuously of Nick's life-style. She had left him when he started writing full time and couldn't afford to keep her in the luxury she was used to. She had gone back home to live with her father in Pinner.

'Writers *need* time to establish themselves,' Jemima said, defending Nick. 'He was a very good writer.'

'His first book took three years to write and made about three thousand pounds,' snorted Lottie. 'I could have understood it if he'd given up his job because he had a success. That's what Ian did after *Bomb Buster* took off. He gave up journalism and—'

'Ian Waring? Did Nick know Ian Waring?' Jemima interrupted.

'He's a very good friend of ours,' said Lottie proudly.

'You've known him a long time?'

'From Cambridge.'

Jemima looked surprised. 'I didn't know Ian Waring had been at Cambridge.'

'That's where I met him.'

'Oh! Which college were you at?'

There was a slight gap in the conversation.

'I was at a secretarial college,' Lottie answered.

Jemima pressed on: 'Did Nick and Ian see a lot of each other?'

Lottie nodded. 'I suppose so. But Nick was very jealous of Ian. It was when Ian got successful that Nick decided he was going to try full-time writing.'

Jemima felt a twinge of shame at her intellectual snobbery. But that emotion disappeared when she looked at the manila folder which she had just removed from the top of one of the filing cabinets. 'The Father-in-Law's Tale', read the writing on the label. Jemima shut the drawer and gave Lottie a very hard, long look.

'Oh, I thought I had looked there,' Lottie said, unconvincingly.

Leaving Lottie to lock up, Jemima took the manuscript and returned to the office. She despatched the manila folder off to Jamie to read and decided to give Cherry a treat. Cherry was to try and find Ian Waring. The girl's nose had not come out from behind *Bomb Buster* since she had bought the paperback. Cherry was a great fan of Ian Waring and was always extolling his virtues to Jemima: he was 'a good read'. Jemima's tastes were more inclined towards the delicately wrought Beckleigh tale than Ian Waring's derring-do.

Ian Waring's success as an adventure writer was one of the publishing phenomena of the past few years. He had only written a couple of books, but had already amassed a fortune based on international sales and film rights. *Bomb Buster* was just about to open as a film in London. Enthusiastically, Cherry set to work tracking down Ian Waring. His extremely pushy, American literary agent, Vic Aaronson, told her that she would find him signing his latest book, *Nukeforce*, in the book department of a West End store. He had just come back from a promotional trip to New York on *Concorde*, and had gone straight on to plug his book in Britain.

Quite fanciable, Cherry thought, as she joined the queue waiting to have their books signed. She guessed he was in his early thirties. He was not classically handsome, but he looked tough and fit, very much the old-fashioned macho type which he wrote about. He smiled and joked, chatting easily to the customers as he inscribed their books.

Cherry had bought two books, one for her and one for Jemima – she still hoped to convert her boss to the delights of his books. Megalith Television could bear the expense, she thought, as she came to the head of the queue and proffered the two copies.

'Who shall I sign this to?' Ian Waring asked, without looking up.

'Just "Cherry".'

'Fine.'

'I'm looking forward to it. I loved *Bomb Buster*,' Cherry enthused.

'Good. And who's this other one for?'

Cherry's enthusiasm for Ian Waring waned when she saw his reaction to Jemima's name. He hadn't so much as glanced up for her, but he inquired with genuine delight about Jemima, and said how pleased he was that she should like his work. Sometimes she wondered gloomily about the value of working for a national celebrity.

Jemima was not very sure why she decided to enlist Ian Waring's help in unravelling the mystery of Nick's death. When he came round to meet her at the office, she did not recognise him from their university days. However, as he explained, he had been one of the rugger hearties whilst she had been one of the stars of the theatrical set, so it was not so surprising that they had not known one another then. He still looked the part, Jemima thought approvingly. He sported the kind of tan that is only gained by plenty of outdoor activity, like skiing – not from lying comatose on a beach. He was wearing a quasi-military combat jacket, but of the most expensive design. She may not have recognised him, but Jemima vaguely remembered hearing the name in connection with a student exploit. 'The Lanehurst Leap', as it had come to be called, entailed jumping from the roof of the college chapel down onto the roof of the dining hall.

'Sheer folly!' Ian laughed. 'Only to be attempted at midnight when completely plastered!'

The thought of Nick and Ian being close friends seemed incongruous, but their friendship stretched further back than college, Ian explained. They had gone to school together, and then on to the same college. They had remained close even when Nick had been posted abroad. Ian was at a loss to understand his friend's death.

Jemima found something rather appealing about Ian's quite blatant delight in his newly acquired riches. His almost child-like enthusiasm for all his exploits took the curse off what might otherwise have seemed an appalling tendency to brag. So, Jemima was not interested only in learning more about Nick when she accepted Ian's invitation to have lunch the following day.

At Jemima's suggestion they went to her old haunt 'L'Aubergine', where Ian entertained Jemima with stories of his adventures. He had ridden racehorses in Ireland for a year, and had spent some time with the paras in Northern Ireland, and with the SAS. But his books depended on a solid research background, he emphasised, which he knew was important from his time spent as a journalist. He was such a lively raconteur that it was with some reluctance that Jemima pulled the conversation back to the subject of Nick.

'I take it you knew his wife,' she said. Jemima always had some interest in the women her one-time lovers married.

'Lovely laundered Lottie!' Ian laughed, explaining that Lottie's father, Maurice Arnold, had bought his daughter respectability. He had bought her Roedean, then a smart finishing school in Switzerland, then an expensive husband-catching secretarial college in Cambridge, where she netted Nick Beckleigh. When Nick entered the Foreign Office, Maurice Arnold had thought he had done very well for his daughter.

Jemima was curious to know why respectability was so important to Maurice Arnold, but she was pleased that she had guessed Lottie to be a phoney.

'In the early days,' Ian explained, 'his money came from dubious sources. Now he owns posh restaurants, but it used to be night clubs and protection rackets.' He looked serious. 'Mr Arnold's empire is riding on the back of some very nasty things, Jemima.'

'Are you sure of your facts?' asked Jemima Shore, Investigator.

'Always,' Ian asserted. 'I started investigating Arnold when I was on the *Mirror*, and I unearthed a whole lot of dirt. But the lawyers got scared, and I was told to lay off the story. Anyway, anything criminal was always done through a fixer, Benny Cope.' Ian paused. He looked across the table, and took hold of Jemima's hands. 'That was all a long time ago, though. I'm more interested in investigating a certain beautiful Investigator sitting opposite me, now.'

Later that day, Jamie reported back to Jemima that he had read the Nick Beckleigh manuscript she had sent him, and that it was dreadful. He was terribly disappointed and would return it straight to Nick's agent to deal with. Jemima had been really excited by the idea that there might be a link between Arnold – given what Ian had told her, and the title of the book – and Nick's death.

Now, that idea was dashed. Jamie had described the book as 'a rather leaden allegory about life in a Dorset village'. Setting off on another train of thought, Jemima asked Jamie to return the manuscript to her. She would have it dated. Hadn't Jamie declared the writing to be not a patch on the previous work? Jemima wondered if the manuscript had somehow been substituted by an earlier piece.

Cherry was sent off on another errand. This time the male target was not such an attractive one as Ian Waring. It was Mr Troyne. He might not be the ideal guest for a drinks party, but Jemima had to thank Miles for putting her in touch with an expert on manuscripts. Just my luck, thought Cherry: Jemima gets Ian Waring; I get Mr Troyne.

She inveigled him to come to Nick Beckleigh's flat, so that he could analyse different examples of Nick's work and date them. In the meantime, Jemima went over to visit Ian in his fashionable apartment in the giant concrete complex of the Barbican in the City of London. The previous day, when he had taken her back there, she had been struck by how much the flat was an extension of his persona. It was ultra modern, with high-tech furniture and all possible electronic gadgets – a word processor, a small computer, a video. One end of his study was a miniature armoury, with several racks of weapons ranging from small hand guns to quite powerful rifles in cages under lock and key. Jemima sensed, somehow, that they were not just for show. The other walls were covered with pictures of Ian as a rowing and rugger blue, and shields for various sporting activities.

Although the furniture and the few *objects d'art* were in exquisite good taste, Jemima suspected that they had been chosen by a firm of interior decorators rather than Ian. He had little direct input into the choice, she felt. His own personality was discernible from the number of machines, from the huge film posters of *Bomb Buster*, and from the numerous pictures of himself. There were photographs of himself with celebrities, amongst the paras, in SAS uniform, and several of the profile that was on the back of his books. It was strange, Jemima thought, how such an entertaining person could live in such an arid – almost fantasy – environment. She had thought initially that he had been quietly sending up the whole macho image, but now she wasn't so sure. Anyway, he had agreed to help her in her search for Nick's murderer.

They would pool resources. Jemima was interested to

share Ian's knowledge of gangland London, and in particular everything he knew about Maurice Arnold. She had one of her hunches that Arnold was the key to the mystery of his son-in-law's death.

Ian poured Jemima a large glass of champagne and they sat together on the black leather sofa under his picture window. He described Arnold's method of operating. Unfortunately, Ian's own contact with the Arnold empire had been found dead in Epping Forest with a bullet through the head. Ian suspected that was courtesy of Arnold. He had been a victim of a contract killing. Jemima's nose twitched. This was the second time in the past few days she had come across contract killing. Some of Cherry's research on Billy Standen suggested that he had underworld connections who were hired killers.

Ian explained the mechanics of contract killings to her. The hit-man frequently did not know who his employer was. He could get paid direct, through a dead letter-box or left luggage office, or – frequently – via a chain of contacts, when the money and details of the job were sent from one address to another, the route changing each time so it would be almost impossible to trace a connection between employer and killer.

When he finished his explanation, Jemima tilted her head and looked at Ian as if she were issuing him a challenge: 'Could we prove Arnold was involved in contract killing?'

Ian looked at her as if he didn't believe what he had just heard. 'Yeah, yeah, and come out with at least both your kneecaps missing,' he remarked sarcastically.

Jemima knew full well that any investigation into mobland could be dangerous, but she wanted to share all the information Ian had gained during his journalist days, and maybe spur him to find out some more.

'Listen Jemima. Back in '78, I got as close as I could,

but I couldn't actually *prove* the link between Arnold and Benny Cope. I could only suspect. I couldn't even find the first link in the chain.'

'Well, I'm going to find it.'

'Jemima,' Ian urged, 'don't go trying any confrontations.'

'No one would hurt little ol' me!' she replied, trying to laugh off his concern. Ian only shook his head. She tried another tack.

'It would make a smash-hit book! You told me all your books were backed up by first-hand research.' Ian looked serious for a moment and nodded.

'You're right Jemima.' Then he laughed, and kissed her. 'But you'll have to be in it too.'

She gave way to the inevitable, and they were lying back in his enormous king-size bed, finishing off the champagne, when the phone rang. It was Cherry, for Jemima. She had finally emerged from the clutches of Mr Troyne with some concrete information about the manuscript. The manuscript in the manila folder was categorically written at least five years before the first novel, and definitely by Nick.

Jemima replaced the phone on the hook and snuggled up to Ian. 'So who had got the real manuscript,' he asked, 'if there ever was one?'

Jemima mused, 'I don't know. Lottie? Or Maurice Arnold, I suppose? But I'm going to find it.'

Ian put his arm round her and looked at her fondly: 'I warn you, though. Don't try any confrontations.'

'Don't worry, I'm not going to,' she replied calmly. Nevertheless, she was determined now to find out something that would dent his masculine assurance, and make him respect her as a professional journalist – rather than the glamorous TV star. 'I have a completely different line of investigation,' she announced.

'What's that?' inquired Ian, his professional curiosity aroused.

'Now Ian,' joked Jemima, 'what sort of journalist reveals his sources.' She gently chided, and turned over to give him her full attention.

It had been hard work getting any information out of Billy Standen. She had to use a mixture of all her charm and a large quantity of alcohol, and even make a vague promise that she would ask him to appear on her programme. There was one moment when she thought he would walk out. This was at the mention of Nick. She could see the murmurings of the anger that had boiled over at her party. It was the name of Benny Cope that calmed him down. He eyed Jemima with a new respect.

'Benny Cope is a very moody man, Miss Shore,' he said.

'Say Benny wanted somebody rubbed out. Have you any idea how he'd start?'

He looked at her cannily. 'I might have a few ideas – if it was background to our programme.' Mentally crossing her fingers, Jemima reassured Billy.

'Well, strictly on the QT and not for publication or television.' Billy continued, and gave Jemima all the background he knew on Cope. Finally, he mentioned the name Denny Sutton – the first link in the contract-killing chain.

Jemima was so delighted to have made such rapid progress that she went straight round to the Barbican to tell Ian in person. She wanted to see his reaction when she told him, rather than speak to him on the telephone. She felt very pleased with herself when a look of amazement crossed his face.

'Are you sure?' he asked.

'We can only find out by asking.'

'Not "we", Jemima.'

'What do you mean?'

Ian walked across the room to his armoury, and took down an automatic. He looked hard at Jemima.

'I am redefining the terms of our partnership. You stick to the investigation. You're good at that – better than I ever thought, Jemima.' She felt a chill for a moment, as he loaded the gun. 'I'll do the rough stuff.'

Jemima spent the rest of that day trying to work on scripts, but she hadn't realised how much she cared for Ian until the doorbell rang late at her flat. A spasm of relief passed through her as she opened the door to find Ian standing there safe and out of danger.

She made them both some coffee, and poured him a brandy and herself a glass of white wine. She then sat down in the pretty Victorian armchair next to her fireplace, and listened to the story of Ian's day. She was as eager to listen as he was to tell it: he was overflowing with excitement.

'I've cracked it Jemima!' he exclaimed. 'I've found the chain of the command, right down to the killer, and right up to Cope.'

'So what happens?' Jemima was as excited as Ian. 'The money gets sent in a package to the first address?'

'That's it. And so on down the line.' Ian strode about the room as he explained how he had started off with the contact that Jemima had given him. He had found Denny Sutton watering down the whisky at the back of his club in Wanstead. A short fat man in his early fifties, Denny had given no resistance, and had soon told Ian the name and address of the next link in the chain.

Ian had to be more aggressive with the next man, who ran a garden nursery in Rotherhithe. Alan Stratton denied anything to do with Cope and it was only under the threat of extremely unpleasant things happening to him that he gave Ian the 'Killer's' address.

'A Mr Lewis is the Killer, Jemima.'

'And what is the going rate?'

'Ten thousand. Now I've got all the background for my book.'

Jemima looked worried: 'You're sticking your neck out seeing this contract killer.'

'He's a businessman. I paid him. I often buy my plots.'

Jemima was unsure whether Ian was being realistic in his casual approach. 'I don't want anything to happen to you,' she said, getting up from her chair and crossing the room to where he stood, looking out of her window. He put his arms round her and held her close.

'I'll be careful. If you knew how much I fancied you at Cambridge. I so much wanted to be part of your world.'

'Well you are now.' Jemima stretched up and kissed him on the mouth.

'Of course what you've found out is fine for your work, but what about justice. All the villains are still at large, and we haven't proved the connection between Benny Cope and Arnold.'

Ian shook his head. 'We know what happened. But we'll never be able to prove it. No one will give evidence.'

That wasn't good enough for Jemima. She was determined, now, to bring Nick Beckleigh's murderer to justice.

The news of Alan Stratton's death made the front page of the afternoon paper the next day. He had been shot dead in his market garden.

Jemima was certain that this was a result of Ian's inquiries, and was unsure what to do next. She was dealing with dangerous people, and did not want either Ian or herself hurt in any way. The best thing, she thought, was to have another chat with Billy.

He didn't seem surprised by what had happened.

'Dead men don't turn grass, Jemima.'

'In cold blood?'

'They holds a tribunal. Depends what picture they got on the video that week. Nature strictly follows art with those mugs. One week it's Brando. Next, it's George Raft. Maurice used to fancy himself as Edward G. in my time.'

Jemima was fascinated, but this didn't seem to help solve Nick's death. 'I must ask you about Nick again,' she plunged in. Billy's eyes narrowed, 'I don't know him, Jemima.'

'Didn't Vee ever bring him back to the flat?'

'She'll get a spanking if she did,' retorted Billy.

'Billy, I'm trying to find out who knew him – about his friends.'

'That's it. He didn't have no friends. He was a loner. He lived for his writing. That's Vee's story, anyway.'

Jemima asked Billy if Vee had mentioned Ian Waring at all. She suddenly felt cold when Billy nodded, and said that Ian had been Nick's mentor, and had read all his work first, before anyone else. The explanation for Nick's death suddenly dawned on Jemima. Everything was not what it seemed. Still, before she jumped to any conclusions, she would have to check some facts.

Vic Aaronson, Nick's agent, was delighted to see Jemima. His client having been seen with Jemima Shore Investigator had made him an even more desirable property than he was already. Jemima, however, was in no mood for small talk. She came straight to the point. Aaronson blinked at her. He really couldn't understand how some of these TV people could be so naive. Yes, Nick's next book was about contract killing. But even with Nick's name he could not sell a book just on an idea. He had had Nick's story outline for several months. It was a terrific story, he assured Jemima. She was certain it was, and accurate in every detail.

She chastised herself mentally. She had let herself be sidetracked by Ian's energy and enthusiasm, and had not seen all the pointers as to what he was really up to. She had to confront him with her suspicions.

Warning Cherry what she was about to do, Jemima drove her Mercedes through the crowded London streets to the Barbican. She parked in one of the concrete bunker-like underground car parks, and went up to the piazza. She strolled past the artificial lake, and contemplated the fountains playing at one end. She took several deep breaths in an attempt to calm herself. Finally, she went up to Ian's flat. He had said he was delighted when she phoned up to say she was coming over. He wouldn't be so delighted when he knew the purpose of her visit.

She found herself icy calm as she faced him. They were both sitting on the leather sofa where they had agreed to be partners and help each other solve Nick's death.

'The research you'd done on Maurice Arnold and Benny Cope gave you the idea for your book,' started Jemima. 'It was to be a crime thriller. Exciting. Very dangerous.'

'*You* suggested it, Jemima!' Ian burst in. He looked totally unfazed by her change of mood.

'No,' persisted Jemima. 'You came up with it, months ago. You knew the theory, but you had to check it actually worked. Ten thousand is nothing to you for a good plot. You put it through Benny Cope's system before you went to the States.'

Jemima felt chilled by Ian's matter-of-fact answer: 'I always get my facts right, Jemima.'

She couldn't believe it. It all seemed unreal.

'Why did you kill him? He was your *friend*.'

It then all came out. Slowly and calmly, but with total hatred. Nick had achieved everything that Ian had ever wanted, with complete ease. Ian had always been the runner-up. It had started at school and continued at university. Nick got a scholarship; Ian got only a place. Even Jemima's brief affair with Nick was another cause for jealousy. (That, thought Jemima, explained Ian's delight when she had showed some interest in him.) What finally broke Ian was Nick's literary success. His wealth and best sellers meant nothing compared to the critical success Nick had achieved. When he read the manuscript of Nick's second novel, Ian knew he would never be able to compete with the quality of work. He set out to destroy him, both physically and critically. He set up the contract killing before he left for the States, so it would take place whilst he was away, and he substituted the manuscript of the novel when he returned. Lottie had, after all, spoken the truth when she said she hadn't found the manuscript. Ian had it. His competitive nature had driven him to the awful, ultimate conclusion of killing his best friend. It was a bitter twist on the David and Jonathan tale.

But why had he agreed to help her? He must have known that she would have found the truth out eventually – as indeed she had. Cherry had once remarked on how Ian's heroes, in his books, seemed oblivious of danger – almost as though they had a kamikaze death-wish. Perhaps Ian had one himself. His explanation fitted everything else Cherry had said about his books. Initially, perhaps, he just wanted to keep in touch with Jemima. Then, it became a challenge – how good an 'Investigator' was she? How close to the edge could he get?

The man had gone over the edge, not just close to it. 'You know we'll have to go to the police,' she said, gently.

'Couldn't we go away together? Escape? You and me, Jemima?'

'No, Ian,' Jemima shook her head. 'This is the real world, not one of your books. You can't get away with murder.'

Slowly, Ian got up from the sofa and crossed the room. Jemima was unsure what he was going to do. Was he going to turn violent? He was most certainly large enough to overpower her without difficulty. Or was it going to be worse? She was only too aware of the battery of arms in the flat. . . .

But all he did was open one of his fitted cupboards, pull out a pile of school exercise books, and hand them to Jemima. She put these in her large satchel-like bag, and led him by the hand, like a small boy, out of the flat.

They had come out of the flats, and had turned down the street towards the car park entrance, when Ian suddenly clutched at his chest. He staggered against the wall, and collapsed in a heap on the pavement. He had been shot in the chest.

Jemima knelt down beside him and cradled him in her arms. She wondered, aloud, if the bullet had been intended for her. 'No, Jemima,' he whispered. 'After Stratton, it had to be me. It's Maurice Arnold. I love you.' Tears welled up out of her eyes as she stroked his forehead. 'Nick's beaten me again.'

'Oh no, not in my eyes,' murmured Jemima insistently as he lay dying in her arms.

*

The revelation that Ian had been the killer, and his subsequent death, upset Jemima more than she cared to admit to anybody. She was also annoyed with herself for not seeing through Ian earlier. The police had taken all Ian's notes, but they held out little hope that they would be able to convict any of the contract chain.

The only comfort to be got out of the whole business was that the manuscript – Nick's genuine new novel, which Ian had given her, was a work of genius. It would secure Nick's reputation for all time, Jamie assured her.

Jemima had next week's show to write.

# The Damask Collection

Everybody in the building had a pet subject, and everybody took every opportunity of plugging it. In her time at Megalith Television, Jemima Shore had been approached by virtually every member of staff with a wonderful idea for her programme. It was high time, said one woman in Accounts, that she got down to an in-depth investigation of single parents whose one-time lovers were now making fortunes in other countries, especially those who had only been doing their best to give foreign businessmen a good opinion of the English way of life: not, she hastened to add, that she had any personal axe to grind here. At least three men from different departments had suggested on at least a dozen different occasions that it was her duty to blow the chicanery of the Inland Revenue wide open. A cameraman longed to make a hard-hitting series entitled 'Eyesores of Britain', but made little progress after insisting that it would have to include the Megalith building.

Even the big boss had a bee in his bonnet. At every programme planning conference Cy would somehow manage to wheedle the discussion round to the subject of wine. If not the greatest of connoisseurs, he was a great inhaler and imbiber. Plans for a feature on the glass industry would turn his conversation to the shapes of wine bottles. A mention of France was bound to lead to a disquisition on claret, so intense that one might have suspected him of seeking an excuse for spending weeks of research in the Bordeaux region. In fact this could have been the case with a junior executive, but not with Cy. Although he was forever dashing off on trips to disturb the peace of contacts in Manchester, New York or Paris, he made a point of never being away for more than a few days at a time: he was too concerned with the threat of someone making a takeover bid for power in his absence.

His interest in the products of the grape was genuine. His perseverance was wearying. Jemima might have guessed from the beam on his frequently dour face as he entered her office one morning that at last he saw that perseverance paying off.

'Feel like a little drink this evening?' He flapped a sheet of paper to and fro. 'All in the call of duty. Splendid wines, interesting company.'

'Cy, I'd love to come for a drink with you, but with these schedules and this –'

'Sorry, not going to be able to make it myself. Flying off to Gateshead.'

'Good Lord, don't you lead a wild and glamorous life!'

'Sweet child.' He was still in a good humour. 'Anyway, the wine tasting's tonight. Wear your loveliest.'

He handed her the sheet of paper and produced a folded catalogue from an inside pocket. Jemima ran her gaze down it. There was nothing outstanding about the presentation: the sort of traditional affair of a kind she had been to several times, this time given by Samuel Pedlar of the Pedlar Cellars, declaring themselves Wine Merchants from the time of George the Third. Inside the catalogue was an appetising list of some splendid vintages. But then, the Pedlars would hardly have gone to this trouble for a mere display of plonk imported in barrel.

She said: 'Come on, Cy, what's this all about?'

'Wine is news, these days. The great growth product. Housewives drink it instead of tea.'

'Don't be devious. What's the story?'

He frowned, as if about to assert his authority; then grinned. 'All right, I've been got at. By a writer called Acton Tindall. The name mean anything to you?'

'Not a thing.'

'Well, he has a story that he thinks would be of great interest to us. About wine.'

Jemima groaned. She had a vision of raking through the ashes — or grape pips — of some hoary old wine shipping scandal. Fake Chianti from Naples made out of old banana skins, or spaghetti left-overs: hadn't it been done to death?

'Mr Tindall,' said Cy solemnly, 'claims to have found the Damask Collection.'

'Great. That's something else that doesn't mean a thing to me.'

Cy looked reproachful. 'The collection is alleged, my dear, to be a choice of perfect vintages spanning the past two hundred years, assembled slowly and secretly over that time. It has been talked about, argued over, dreamed about — but no one has ever proved that it exists. If it does, it's priceless, like a legendary collection of stamps. I see it as a plug for the wine programme we've always wanted to do.'

'We, Cy?' Jemima protested. '*You!*'

'Come on, now. You like wine. Go along and indulge that sensitive palate.'

'Cy, all he wants is publicity.'

'Quite normal. Oh, and if there are any bottles going spare I'm interested in the Palmer '53 – but the '61 will do.'

By the time she had left the office the banks had been closed for more than two hours. Jemima was retrieving her cash dispenser card and scooping up the crisp fivers from outside the local branch when a hand fell on her shoulder.

'Don't move.'

She stood petrified. It was what she had often feared would happen. Surprising, really, that it did not happen more often. There you were, with your handbag open, the card in one hand and money in the other: just asking to be robbed.

'Don't scream,' said the gruff voice. 'Just turn round. Very slowly.'

She turned. The card slid through her fingers. As those remembered, heavily sensual lips closed on hers she flung her arms round his neck. She wanted to call him a swine for frightening her like that; wanted to punch him where it would hurt; but wanted even more to have his arms round her. Even though it was all over, all a thing of the past, he was still a pretty substantial memory.

Now the evening might turn out to be more than just a chore. Collecting her dispenser card and a wayward fiver which showed signs of wanting to emulate a wind-blown leaf, she put her arm through his and led him away down the street.

'Max, you won't mind waiting while I bath and change?'

'I'll wait while you bath, but do you have to change?'

'I've got an invitation.'

'After all this time, I need one?' His whisper of an East End accent mocked her and perhaps mocked him-self. His clothes had obviously been designed to his own taste – and that taste was as brash and bright as it had ever been.

She might have known how it would end up.

As she struggled up out of the tangled sheets and crumpled pillow, and pushed away his hand to make it clear that there was no time for an encore, she said:

'Look, I have this invitation. An exclusive wine tasting to which are only invited guests chosen for their wit, charm and knowledge of the good life.'

His fingers found and stroked her thigh. 'So how are you going to sneak me in?'

'I'll lie about you, as usual. Come on, let's get ready. All right, it's a bore – I'm only going because it's work, but –'

'That was always the trouble, wasn't it? In our brief but glossy relationship. You were always out working while I was at home doing the cooking.'

She kissed his nose and sprawled her way out of bed. Very beautifully had he cooked, she thought; and made a meal out of quite a few other things. Even a snack like this evening's had been done with style and grace. Now, whether he liked it or not, she had work to do. She hoped he would like it. His company would provide a refreshing aftertaste to whatever was solemnly poured into the undoubtedly exquisite glasses.

It occurred to her that, as one of the slickest entrepreneurs and wheeler-dealers in all the continents so far known to man, Max Highams might know something about the fabled Damask Collection. On the other hand, he might think it was something to do with the rag trade, one of the few markets he had never dabbled in. Not worth the effort of asking. With Max, only one effort had really been worth it – and that, while it lasted, had certainly been worth every sob and sigh.

'And now,' she said crisply, 'we get down to the real business of the evening.'

'If you're going to tell me that that wasn't –'

'Get dressed. You've got ten minutes.'

'Who *is* this whatever, or whoever, we've got to meet?' he grumbled.

The whatevers and whoevers were already assembled in appreciative numbers when Jemima led him into the house in Milton Gardens and down the steps into the private cellar. Not, she thought, just a basement like everybody else's – or what some advertisers called a 'spacious garden flat' – but a true, extensive, richly stocked cellar. Racks of wine bottles shielded the walls. Voices, however hushed, struck religious resonances from the ceiling like the devotions of a monastic choir. Down the centre of the vault was a long table on which bottles were arranged in groups and glasses waited for nectar to be poured in and for susceptible noses to be dipped marginally in. There were large flagons on each table for the tasters to tip out the residue after their pernickety sipping. She hoped Max would not, out of sheer bravado, pick up one of the dreg collectors and swill it back at one go; and then, mischievously, half hoped he would do just that to shatter the solemnity.

'Miss Shore!' An unctuous voice caught Jemima as she was sniffing the bouquet of a fruity Pommard. 'It *is* Jemima Shore, isn't it?'

The man on the other side of the table must have been around forty, and from the smoothness of his tan had evidently spent a lot of time recently in the sun. His suit was a casual lightweight, but he himself was more than a fraction overweight.

His plump, epicene hand reached vainly out above the bottles. 'Miss Shore, I was told you might well be here.'

'Our only reason for coming, in fact,' said his companion obsequiously. He was built in an even larger mould and had a sagging, crumpled look about him.

Max raised his eyes from contemplation of the small print at the bottom of a label. 'Hello, Ira. What's the game this year? Thought you'd sunk without trace in Capri.'

The larger man's puffy features crumpled even further, as if a very large hand had squashed down on them. 'Well, if it isn't Max. And you – I thought *you* were living abroad, too. Singapore, or somewhere.'

'Just passing through.'

'Well. Yes. Well, then. Er, Miss Shore, may I introduce a friend and colleague, the distinguished author, Acton Tindall?'

Since there was no possibility of achieving a handshake across the table, the two men began plodding towards the end in order to come round.

Jemima sipped her wine, and murmured over the rim of the glass: 'Tweedle-Dum and Tweedle-Dee. And you know Dum, then?'

'Ira Bartholomew,' said Max. 'Top quality phoney.'

'You're sure?'

'Certain.'

'When they get here, let me have ten minutes alone with them.' She thought with malicious pleasure of what she would have to say to Cy if she could prove he had been conned.

The men arrived, both starting to talk effusively at once. Max surveyed them with a curl of his fleshy lower lip, then pretended to recognise someone at the far end of the table and drifted off.

'Now,' said Jemima briskly, 'you want to sell me a story.'

'Oh, not sell, dear lady.' Ira Bartholomew spread his hands in reproof. 'Well, not entirely.'

'We need your co-operation.' Tindall took over. 'And you're going to be fascinated.' He nodded towards an unoccupied table, one of several supplied with glasses and a wine coaster, in a corner of the room. 'Shall we sit down for a few minutes?'

Jemima settled herself as comfortably as possible on a narrow, hard-backed chair, and waited for what Acton Tindall assured her would be a tale of romance, adventure, mystery . . . absolutely everything in it.

Eagerly interrupted from time to time, Tindall told his story in a rhapsodic prose which boded ill for the quality of the books he wrote. Jemima was used to dramatic exaggerations, however. In her profession she dealt every day with people wanting to decorate and inflate their personal background and career. She knew what to discard and what to select. Certainly there did seem to be a genuinely exciting history behind Tindall's flourishes and Bartholomew's earnest interjections.

What it boiled down to was that Tindall and his friend claimed to have tracked down part of the legendary hoard of wines known as the Damask Collection. Before the Second World War it had been the prize possession of the Baron de Maurance, cherished and well guarded in his château by the Loire. Then came the War, and the Nazis. Before they arrived, the Baron had packed up a significant proportion of his collection and despatched it into the safe keeping of his old friend Samuel Pedlar. Unfortunately he had left the operation until almost too late: the invaders smashed into his comfortable world before he could shift the rest of his treasure. And after the War there was no one to seek out and claim the vintages which had been salvaged. The de Maurance family being Jewish, most of them perished in concentration camps. The estate was broken up when there was no one to inherit. Old Mr Pedlar, secretive about the extent of the collection which had been entrusted to his care, had been equally secretive about his attempts to trace a possible heir. Growing older and feebler, living the life of a recluse and not knowing how long this life would last, he wanted to know before he died that there was in fact a living heir, somehow, somewhere.

'And we' – Ira Bartholomew could not restrain himself – 'have found that heir.'

'And with Ira's guidance,' said Tindall, 'I have been writing a book about the search, from start to finish.'

'Which you want me to publicise,' said Jemima.

Bartholomew spoke for his friend and himself. It was obviously a habit of his. Whoever had set this whole saga in motion, it had not been the somewhat nervous, lethargic Tindall. 'We are men of business, Miss Shore. It's to our mutual advantage. Publicity and therefore some profit, yes. Naturally. And for yourself, you have an exciting programme, culminating in the meeting of old Mr Pedlar with the heir he has been searching for.'

'You've given him any hint about this?'

'At the moment he stays in bed and will see nobody. But perhaps when you are ready to approach him, and –'

'Can I see this book?'

Tindall exchanged a triumphant glance with his partner. 'I'll send you round the manuscript, as far as I've got.'

'It's not finished?'

'How can it be, Miss Shore?' said Bartholomew. 'You and Mr Tindall, and myself, are going to complete the last chapter.'

'Oh,' said Jemima dubiously, 'we are, are we?'

Twenty minutes later she was giving Max Highams a précis of the story. In telling it over again, she found her own interest was increasing. Even if it was only half true, the tale was one with undoubted appeal for her regular audiences. Trying to keep a cool head, she asked Max just how much he really knew about Ira Bartholomew and the likelihood of it all being some weird fantasy.

They were approaching the Trattoria Lyrica as he delivered his verdict. 'Had his fingers in a lot of pies. Sails pretty close to the wind. Not exactly a crook, but quite a con-man.'

'So you don't think that story is true? I mean, why would they dream up something like that?'

'The trouble with con-men is that you never do know if they're telling the truth or not,' said Max, 'and most of the time, neither do they.'

They reached the restaurant and went in to a greeting of a bouquet less subtle than that of the wines they had been tasting: an aroma compounded of roast baby lamb, aubergines, cannelloni, oregano, garlic, coffee and a spirit burner. Then there was Carlo, breathing a welcome over them and adding a soupçon of some pine-y Italian cologne.

'Meester Highams, long time we don't see you.'

'I'm living in Singapore just now.'

'You crazy? All that foreign food!'

Carlo took Jemima's coat and smiled knowingly at her and then at Max. Just like old times, said his smirk. Jemima had not been here since Max left, and was not sure they ought to have come here now. A tag scampered across her mind: 'Where'er we tread, 'tis haunted, holy ground.'

'Your guest is waiting,' said Carlo, starting to lead the way across the restaurant. 'Or perhaps he play the host, yes?'

'Oh, no,' breathed Jemima.

At a table against the wall sat Acton Tindall.

'You wouldn't like to go to a nice quiet Wimpy Bar, would you?' said Max.

It was too late. Tindall was getting to his feet, flapping that same limp hand at Jemima and waving her to a chair.

She did not even attempt a smile. 'But how did you know . . .?'

His own smile was complacent. 'It seemed a pity to break off our chat so soon. I heard you mention this place. And I wanted to bring you some evidence. I could tell you were not entirely convinced. Ira sometimes pitches it a bit too strongly, doesn't he?'

'Evidence?' said Jemima.

'Please. Sit down, we'll order, and then you will have some proof.'

It was tantalising. Jemima could tell Max wanted to storm out of the place and take her somewhere else. She was more than half minded to fall in with that. Yet there was still that feeling of hers that a good story might come out of this, a good programme. It was her job. She had to go through with it.

She sat down.

Carlo took an order for smoked salmon, *osso bucco*, one of his special fillets, and then revealed that Acton Tindall had already ordered – and would be footing the entire bill.

Max glared.

'You like to order the wine now?' Carlo concluded.

Tindall shook his head. 'I've brought the wine. On which I'll pay full corkage.'

Carlo's glare could have given Max a few tips; but with an angry shrug he went off.

'As I said, I heard you mention the name of this restaurant at the wine tasting.' Tindall leaned back smugly in his seat. 'I wanted to speak to you on my own. And –

as I've said — I wanted to offer you a precious piece of evidence.'

He groped under the table and with the greatest care lifted out a leather-covered box with a handle at the side. When he set it on the table, the box sat at an angle.

Irritated by this protracted business, Jemima said sharply: 'Mr Tindall, I can't recall the titles of any books you may have written.'

'I use several names.' He produced a small key and unlocked the box. 'Under my own name, a novel called *The Domino Set* had some — er — success.'

The box folded out to reveal an old bottle with a dusty, torn label. Jemima leaned forward to read it: 'Margaux 1884'.

'Until I found this bottle,' said Tindall in a hushed tone, 'it was thought that the remains of the Damask Collection had gone for ever. This was my first lead.' He took up the story with the quivering enthusiasm Jemima had experienced earlier this evening. 'Trying to get the remainder of his collection out of the country, the Baron had only a young boy to help him. A boy who knew nothing of the value of what he was packing. I found that boy — a middle-aged man now, of course — and he sold me this bottle. Everything else had been drunk or smashed by the barbarians when they looted the estate. But this one he had taken with him as a keep-sake, in memory of the Baron. Now.' He had another object beside him: a camera, equipped with a flash. This he passed across the table to Max. 'A couple of shots of me and Miss Shore together as I pull the cork. Right?'

'You're not going to open it!' cried Jemima. 'You can't! Why?'

'Because, Miss Shore, I always believe in taking out insurance against every eventuality.'

Max took the camera, grinning. 'You mean you don't trust Ira.'

'I don't entirely trust anybody. But I'll be the only man in the world absolutely known – proved – to have drunk from the Damask Collection. Ready?'

Max cheerfully took three or four shots as Tindall lovingly drew the cork and handed it to Jemima. 'A memento.'

Jemina watched as he gently poured from the bottle into his glass. The wine was a bit brown in colour, but after a hundred years or so she supposed that was not surprising. When Tindall held the glass out to her she sniffed; and made a face. Not a good year, she thought wryly; but it was history.

Tindall waited for Max to aim the camera again, and then with ritual slowness drank from the glass. To make sure that there were no slip-ups on the pictures, he indicated that Max should keep shooting, while he drained the last drop of the wine.

Carlo came disapprovingly back with their starters.

Before the plates could be set on the table, Tindall began to get up. His face had gone ashen. He clawed at the air, his eyes widening in agony but seeing nothing. When he fell, he sprawled across the table and scattered glasses and that precious, incomparable bottle.

Max bent over the huddled heap on the floor; turned the head; looked into those staring but no longer agonised eyes.

'That wasn't very good insurance,' he observed, after feeling for a pulse. 'He's dead.'

Jemima spent longer in the Trattoria Lyrica than she had intended. The police had a lot of questions to ask, and she had to be careful about certain answers. Until she knew what had to be done about the Damask Collection, she was not going to spray random remarks about the place.

In spite of that dismal experience, she was back next morning, only to find a police car back in place outside the restaurant; and to catch a glimpse of a plump figure which could only be that of Ira Bartholomew, scuttling away at a speed which threatened to give him a heart attack.

She had come back for her coat, left behind in the aftermath of Tindall's death. Before she could ask for it, Carlo treated her to a dramatic tenor aria full of lamentation.

'Is it good for trade I have the guest poisoned in my restaurant? I am till dawn with the police, I come back in the morning, and what now I got? I got a burglary.'

Jemima looked round the usually discreetly lit, glossily arranged restaurant. Two tables were at the moment on their sides, and the trolley of fruit had been upset all over the floor.

'Did the police say it was poison?' she asked.

'Sure, they take the bottle away; they tell me today. Is poison. Well, sure it's poison. I don't know no wine kill you that quick. It takes years.'

Jemima thought of Ira Bartholomew, in such a hurry to be away. 'That fat man who just left:' she said, 'what did he want.'

'He hear his friend have a heart attack here, he come to pick up any of his things. Anything, wants to see where he sits, everything.'

'And my coat – I suppose your burglars helped themselves to that?'

'But that's it!' wailed Carlo. 'They take nothing. Not even the five pounds Bruno leave in the drawer to bet on the horses. So where's the profit in burglary? Must be a hobby.'

Jemima left in pensive mood. From the start she had felt there was something wrong, but only in a confused, elusive way. Now a new dimension had been added. Murder was quite a dimension.

So, when she got back to her flat, was the mess that faced her. She, too, had had a burglary. Drawers had been opened, chairs tipped over, and her box files emptied out all over the floor. Her jewel case had been up-ended, but nothing was missing. It was sickening; she felt defiled, as if not just the flat but her own body had been fingered and besmirched; but at least no vandal had sprayed aerosol paint all over the walls, which was all too common a pastime these days.

She set an armchair back to rights and sat in it, pondering. When people get murdered, she thought, there's a reason for it, no matter how odd. There must even be a reason, however far-fetched, for burgling a place and taking nothing. But when someone was murdered and then two places got burgled and nothing was taken from either of them . . . there had to be a quite different reason for that.

Looking for something? Or putting something there?

Creepily she wondered, for no obvious reason, what she had done with that cork which Tindall had given her as a souvenir of his bottle of Margaux.

Max, when she asked him, could not remember noticing where she had put it away, or thrown it away. Asked about Ira Bartholomew, he had a bit more to offer. None of it was too blatantly criminal, but there was a hint of shady dealings in various parts of the world. Sometime in the 1970s – this suddenly came back to Max – there had been something fishy about a couple of Modiglianis bought by Ira for a client in the United States: very good Modiglianis, apart from the minor defect of having been painted half a century after Modigliani died.

'Yeh, around 1970,' Max recollected. 'About the time that joker was cooking up that fake Howard Hughes biography.'

'Really?' said Jemima quietly.

Fake biography . . .? Alarm bells rang in her always receptive, resonant mind.

She asked Cherry to do a bit of research; and told Cy that she had grave doubts about the validity of a programme on wine which involved a curious death, conceivably a murder, two burglaries, a legendary collection of historical vintages whose survival had yet to be proved, a long-lost claimant whom she had not yet met, and an unfinished book on a search covering many years and perhaps twisting many facts.

Cy, unwilling to admit he had sent her off on an unrewarding trail, advised patience and further research, and got out of the office before she could summon up the right words in the right order. Cherry, more helpfully, came up with what there was to know about the deceased Acton Tindall. It was little enough. A lousy writer who wanted to write, loved the idea of being a celebrated writer, but lacked one essential ingredient – the ability to write. Two publishers had dealt with him; both had been glad to drop him. Only one of his books had managed to get its royalty advance and production costs back: a mildly salacious novel called *The Domino Set*, dealing with life among the jet set in Ibiza. It appeared that the author had lived there between 1969 and 1971.

Jemima made up her mind. 'Let's get Bartholomew in.'

'What shall I tell him?' asked Cherry.

'Tell him,' said Jemima, 'I'm going to do his programme.'

★

The interior of Cottle's wineshop was as dark and old-fashioned as the exterior, with its gleaming black wood-work and florid gilt lettering, but just as clean and well polished. There were as few bottles on display in the discreet window as there would be dresses on display in a first-rate couturier's. If you dealt with Cottle's you knew what you wanted and what you could expect – the best of its kind. That applied as much to the quality of old Mr Cottle's advice as to his actual stock in hand.

To Jemina, kissing her cheek and escorting her cere-moniously to a chair with one skeletal but firm hand on her arm, he said: 'I was thinking how nice it would be to have a glass of sherry. But how much nicer to have one with a dear and very beautiful friend. You'll have white wine, I know.' He reached for a decanter and peered happily into the golden glow within. 'And why am I granted the pleasure of seeing you today?'

Jemima took the slim crystal glass she was offered, and drank appreciatively. Then she said: 'I want you to tell me about the Damask Collection.'

Mr Cottle chuckled. 'My dear child, what have you been reading?'

'What is the Damask Collection?' she persisted.

'A dream.'

'Go on, tell me.'

A tall case clock in the corner emitted a slow, mellow chime. Mr Cottle listened to it with his head on one side, as if to a favourite piece of music. 'An ideal,' he said ruminatively when it had finished. 'A measurement. It's said that it was the finest collection of wines ever made, over a period of two hundred years.'

That at least confirmed what she had already been told. 'But would the wine be drinkable after all that time?'

'Much of it would be, but it was never really meant to be drunk. That would deplete the collection.'

In spite of his apparent dismissal of the whole thing as a dream, Mr Cottle obviously revelled in the colourful details of the legend. He told her how the collection was supposedly started in the eighteenth century, expanded and passed on secretly on the death of each custodian so that no outsider would ever know where it was. Each inheritor could add a few bottles of what, in his opinion, was the finest vintage of his lifetime, and could discard others if he thought his choice to be better. At his death he willed the lot to the person whose opinion he valued as much as his own. Since each successor trusted the previous custodian, everyone knew the collection to be the finest, and each individual item in it the finest. If there were no additions during a custodian's lifetime, one would know that the wine of that period had not been worthy of the company it was expected to keep. It was a measurement of wine; and a measurement of trust.

'And,' concluded Mr Cottle, 'it doesn't exist.'

Jemima flinched. It had been a lovely build-up to a thumping let-down. 'As the most respected authority on wine in this country, would you be prepared to go into a court of law and swear it doesn't exist?'

'It would be a tragedy to have to stand in a witness-box on oath, and have to deny romance. But under pressure I would be prepared to swear that no one, living or dead, has ever *seen* the Damask Collection.'

'Could I ask you, though, if an 1884 Château Margaux which I saw opened last night would have been worthy of inclusion in the Damask Collection, if such a collection existed?'

He shook his greying head decisively. 'Never. It was the time of the great vine plagues. The '84 was so poor it nearly all had to be swilled down the drain.'

'*Phylloxera?*' breathed Jemima.

Mr Cottle nodded and shuddered. The mere mention of that dreaded disease in this setting was like an invocation of the Devil. To a vigneron it was indeed the Devil incarnate: the *phylloxera vastatrix*, an aphid which invaded France from England in the 1860s and gobbled up the vineyards – including Margaux.

In which case, marvelled Jemima, what wine had Acton Tindall really been drinking – and more to the point, where did it come from?

She could hardly wait to put a few searching questions to Ira Bartholomew.

He arrived at her office with a case which she supposed, for a moment, might contain an assortment of further improbable vintages. Instead he produced a set of slides taken, he gushingly explained, from original photographs. They would be used to illustrate the book – that book which, unfortunately, the poor lamented Tindall could not now complete, but for which he could easily find another writer.

Cherry set up the projector and screen, while Jemima covertly studied Bartholomew. He seemed very sure of himself; but then, a good con-man would have to look sure of himself every time he stepped out on stage.

His running commentary was clear and persuasive. Here a picture of the château, here the Baron de Maurance in happier times, and here one of the Baroness – a beautiful woman in her late thirties, with a radiant smile and a radiant diamond necklace. It was difficult, and sickening, to visualise the two of them humiliated and thrown into the terrors of an extermination camp. But here were photographic records of the Zwickhausen camp near Paderborn – not the final destination of the Baron and Baroness, but a place where their eldest son, Jean-Louis, had been taken.

Ira Bartholomew edged close to the screen to point out one significant line on a faded open page. It listed Jean-Louis Maurance. On the next slide, again of a document in the same format, was the name of Maria Luce Taviani.

'Names from the same records,' he said, 'entered at different times during the same year. She was an Italian girl who had got caught up in the war and had ended up in Zwickhausen. And here' – another page, and the name of Jean-Louis Taviani – 'the name of the child of Jean-Louis Maurance and Maria Luce Taviani, born one year later in the camp.' Bartholomew allowed himself a dramatic pause. 'Armed with an address and a name from a good friend of mine, I went to Yavne in Israel, and there found . . .' He nodded to Cherry, who obediently stabbed the button for the next slide.

It showed a well set-up man who might be in his seventies but was obviously in the peak of physical condition. This man, according to Bartholomew's unwavering narrative, was a survivor of Zwickhausen who remembered Jean-Louis and the Taviani girl. He also remembered that Jean-Louis had died three months before the girl had had her baby, which was probably why the child was recorded in the mother's name. It took some time to track that child into the present, but the quest proved worth it: Bartholomew had discovered that after the war the mother and son had been repatriated to Italy, where within three years she died.

The orphan, with no other family, was taken in by the Sisters of Charity near Orvieto. He was still there – as gardener.

'And Jean-Louis Taviani,' said Ira Bartholomew throbbingly, 'is Jean-Louis Maurance, heir to the Damask Collection. And direct descendant of the first Baron and Baroness de Maurance.'

The final picture, an impressive rounding-off to the story, was an eighteenth-century painting of a man and woman in rich attire, the woman with the same necklace which had already been shown on the neck of the doomed twentieth-century Baroness.

As the lights went up, Bartholomew managed a modest smile. 'That was but a brief resumé of many years' work. I think you'll agree it's a fascinating story.'

'Fascinating,' said Jemima thoughtfully. 'Now, Mr Tindall's manuscript, as far as it went – do you think I could borrow it?'

'But naturally. And these documents, you have a look through them as well. Anything else, you've only to ask.'

Jemima took the loosely bound typewritten pages home with her, leaving instructions with Cherry that she was to be telephoned only in dire emergency; and that wild off-the-cuff inspirations of Cy or pessimistic panics from Guthrie were not to be regarded as emergencies.

The more she read, the more impressed she was. Acton Tindall's writing was lousy – there was no other word for it, or if there was she didn't care to use it – but the facts behind the book all added up. Bartholomew's documentation of his search for the Maurance heir was impeccable. He might have been a rogue during a large part of his career, but even rogues got entangled in truth every now and then.

Yet there were some niggling questions. Although she could let herself be convinced that Bartholomew had genuinely traced the Maurance descendant, she could not understand why he needed Tindall's long-winded book about the Damask Collection. Pedlar would reward him well for the discovery of a Maurance heir. The legendary wine treasure and Tindall's chapters about it were irrelevant.

The doorbell jolted her out of her reverie.

Max said: 'They told me you were working at home.'

'They shouldn't have done.'

'I've come to ask you if you'd like to join me in a late lunch. Oh, and I've got something for you.' He dipped into his jacket pocket and produced a cork.

Jemima's hostility towards her uninvited caller evaporated. 'Where was it?'

'Very nearly in the dry cleaners. I found it in the jacket I was wearing that night. I must have picked it up when the corpse fell in the soup.'

Jemima kissed him lightly, then backed quickly away before he could misinterpret this.

'Don't tell me you're actually coming out to lunch?' said Max.

'In an hour, darling. First I've got to call on my wine merchant.'

One might almost have thought that in the hours between their last meeting and this, Mr Cottle had not moved from his chair. His expression was as sceptical as before, and grew even more so as he turned the cork between his thumb and forefinger. He was reading its markings as a ballistics expert might read the marks on a bullet.

'Not from the Damask Collection?' Jemima ventured.

'Certainly not. This cork was put into a bottle on the estate of Baron de Maurance in 1940. It's all there.' He handed the cork back to her. 'I knew him well,' he said wistfully. 'Fine fellow. I've cracked a few superb bottles of his wine in my time.'

'Mr Cottle, will you do me a great favour?'

'If I can.'

'I believe you know Mr Samuel Pedlar.'

'Founder members of the Saintsbury Club, my dear.

One of my oldest business rivals, and one of my fondest friends.'

'I want you to make an appointment for me to go and see him.'

Mr Cottle's smile faded. Gravely he shook his head. 'That's one thing I can't do. I can't even get to see him myself. The old tick won't even answer my letters. Quite gaga, I guess.'

'Please, Mr Cottle. I'd like you to ring his butler and say I believe I have found the whereabouts of Baron de Maurance's heir.'

Cottle's eyes widened. He appeared to be on the verge of telling her she was on the trail of another silly myth. Then he cleared his throat, heaved himself from his chair, and pottered off to a cramped cupboard between the shop and living room.

Late that afternoon Jemima and Ira Bartholomew were back in the Milton Gardens wine vaults. Again the projector cast its evidence on to a screen. Again Bartholomew told his story, almost word for word the same. That convincing fluency of his was beginning to worry Jemima. She still believed . . . wanted to believe . . . and yet . . .

'Very interesting.'

The dry, papery-thin voice croaked from the huddle of blanket and shrunken shoulders which was Samuel Pedlar, hunched into his wheel-chair and peering out along the vault.

'There are further proofs, sir.' Bartholomew fawned over the old man. 'I'm entirely at your service, sir.'

Max, standing protectively beside Jemima, made an audible sniff.

Pedlar whispered: 'You think you have found the grandson of Baron de Maurance.'

'And the Damask Collection?' added Jemima.

'I believe so.'

'Inigo Cottle says it doesn't exist.'

Pedlar's head rose shakily, gleaming in the light like a bare skull. 'Cottle does, does he? If he knew anything, he'd know I was caretaker to the nearest thing that could be called part of it that has ever existed. Show them, Puckeridge.'

His butler moved deferentially out of the shadows at the end of the vault and went to a grilled wine bin. He opened its massive padlock and swung back the grille. There were at most twenty ancient bottles inside.

'In perfect condition,' cackled Pedlar. 'Five each of the *premiers crus* – Lafite the Seigneur, Margaux the poet, Latour the maestro and Haut-Brion the parfit gentil knight. Such a quartet! The supreme vintages, never to be repeated.'

Only twenty bottles, thought Jemima. Aloud she said: 'You weren't searching for any Damask Collection, were you, Mr Bartholomew?'

'My dear young woman, my business is with Mr Pedlar. I'm grateful for your assistance in facilitating this introduction, but until we do the programme –'

'You don't need a programme now,' said Jemima, 'or a partner. You knew Tindall's bottle of wine was poisoned.' Before he could recover, she went on remorselessly: 'That's why you had my flat and the restaurant burgled. You had to get the cork back. If the cork was put in in 1940, then the poison was put in before the cork that sealed it, and no one could accuse you of Tindall's murder.'

Pedlar was cackling again, more raucously than before.

'You're talking of the notorious '84?'

'The bottle belonged to Tindall,' said Ira Bartholomew. 'No one can accuse me of murder, I've never murdered anyone, I –'

'A lethal vintage indeed.' Old Simon Pedlar was enjoying himself hugely. 'Don't you know the tale? Oh, one of the great black jokes.' His rasp of laughter echoed eerily down the vault. 'As you'll have gathered, Maurance sent his finest claret for me to look after, for his family. But he was forced to leave the rest. All pre-phylloxera vintages and very fine. Too fine for Hitler's thugs. So what did he do? He had just time to place poisoned bottles in every bin, hoping the German officers would drink their fill. And they did.'

'And the false labels on impossible vintages,' Jemima realised, 'were a warning . . .'

'To his friends. To all true friends of wine. A pity your friend wasn't as well informed.'

Ira Bartholomew was crumpling in on himself. He groped for excuses. 'Employing the Damask legend was Tindall's idea entirely. It's his own damn fault he didn't discover the bottle was spiked. Typical. His research always was slipshod. I didn't kill him, and even without the benefit of the cork, the police had written me off. But good riddance to him, anyway.'

'You needed Tindall's book about the Damask Collection as a front,' said Jemima reflectively. 'A decoy to your fraud –'

'Fraud?' said old Pedlar sharply.

'Your precious clarets are not all they seem, Mr Pedlar.' The sequence of pictures began to make sense. The whole well-documented, well-slanted story was making sense. 'I can explain if you will allow me to open one.'

'Outrageous idea.'

Jemima crossed to the projector, bathed the screen in light again, and flicked through the slides until she came to the picture of the Baroness wearing her necklace.

Max Highams said: 'Now, that's something I do know something about. You lot are thinking of the de Maurance name in connection with wine. For me it means diamonds. Pieces of theirs have been turning up since the war, but never the Maurance necklace: twenty Brazilian diamonds of matchless brilliance.'

'Twenty,' Jemima intoned. 'Twenty bottles of claret. And if the corks have been tampered with –'

'Who'd want to tamper with the corks?' spluttered Pedlar.

'Someone who wanted to insert the diamonds. Turn the wine to vinegar, maybe. But think of the profit margin!'

Ira Bartholomew was mopping his face with a large silk handkerchief and, Jemima was positive, thinking about just that – the profit margin.

Pedlar let out a little whimper. Then he creaked into a new position in his wheel-chair, and said in anguish: 'Very well. Open one, Puckeridge. Make it the Haut-Brion. But gently, now.'

As the cork came out with the faintest, most decorous of plops, Jemima went on watching the wretched Bartholomew. He had accused his dead sidekick, Tindall, of being slipshod; but he, too, had made his fatal mistake. It ought to have struck her sooner that there was something missing from all that documentation of his: bags of background stuff, bags of authenticity, but although he had padded out the references to paintings, the Louis Quinze furniture, and the layout of the château in minute detail, there had been no mention whatsoever of the family jewels.

Max's hand was outstretched to receive the cork. He took an eyeglass from a little velvet sachet and pressed it to his eye.

'Hello. Beeswax. And here . . .'

He dipped into his pocket. They held their breath as he took out a knife with a pair of tweezers opening from one end.

'Oh.' Even Max's boisterousness was subdued to a murmur. 'Oh, you little beauty. Oh, what a stone!'

Jemima silently challenged Bartholomew.

'I've spent most of my life convincing people that everything is possible. And I nearly convinced myself, this time. By the time I'd finished talking about the Damask Collection I almost believed it did exist. But then I cottoned on to the diamonds . . .' He was reaching for his coat. 'I wanted a pension. I hoped the heir might be grateful.'

'There is no heir, Mr Bartholomew,' said Samuel Pedlar.

Bartholomew waved indignantly towards the projector. 'Okay, so the rest of it may not have been true, but I swear *that* stuff is for real.'

'It has become another legend,' the husky voice rustled on, 'that I have been searching for the heir to the Baron's title. That is not true. I do, however, accept your evidence, Mr Bartholomew.'

'Then you agree that in the end I've found –'

'There cannot be a claimant to the Baron's title. He was one of my dearest friends, and I know. I know that he was both impotent and sterile. The only child the Baroness gave birth to was not fathered by the Baron. A fact which he understood quite well. That boy was not in the direct line. Nor could his own son be. Nevertheless, Mr Bartholomew, I would like to meet this discovery of yours.'

Jemima burst out impulsively: 'So the reason the Baron sent the diamonds to *you* was because he knew who the father . . . because the father was . . .'

'Mr Bartholomew,' Pedlar interrupted her, 'I will pay you what you ask to bring that man to this country . . . to me.'

Bartholomew looked incredulous; then besottedly grateful. 'I shall fly out tonight. You may rely on me, sir.'

Pedlar waved a dismissive hand. 'And now, Puckeridge. How *has* that wine fared?'

'It seems eminently drinkable, sir.'

'Maurance could always recork a bottle. Mm. Pour it, Puckeridge. With reverence.'

As Pedlar reached for the glass from his butler's hand and raised it to his lips, Jemima let out a cry of alarm. Pedlar merely shook his head, drank and sighed with pleasure.

'Fear not, young lady. The Baron would not have poisoned this vintage.'

There was no Acton Tindall waiting for them in the Trattoria Lyrica this time. The tables stood the right way up, Carlo's aplomb had been restored, and there seemed little likelihood of anyone bringing in and pouring from dubiously ancient bottles.

Jemima was in a mood to relax. As a companion in such relaxation she favoured Max Highams; who was conveniently at the same table.

'You're not really going back tomorrow?'

'I'd have to ask my boss,' he said.

'Who is your boss?'

'A bit of a rough diamond.' He put his hand possessively across the table and covered hers. 'I'm self-employed, as you very well know,' he laughed.

'Ask him in the morning.' Then Jemima raised her eyes, responsive to a flicker of movement in the doorway. 'Oh, no!'

Cy weaved his way between the tables, and took possession of Jemima's spare hand.

'Congratulations, my gorgeous. Marvellous story. Of course we'll do it. A genuine, old-fashioned, way-out scoop. I'm going to buy you dinner.'

Max said: 'I'd already arranged to –'

'Is the food here all right, or should we go somewhere else?'

Carlo's good humour showed signs of deteriorating around the edges.

Jemima said: 'Cy, this is Max Highams. Max, this is my boss. One of the advantages of being self-employed, you'll agree?'

'*Va bene, maestro,*' boomed Cy. '*Va bene.* We stay. But let's have a bottle of your oldest Barolo, if you've got that kind of cellar.'

Carlo seethed. Still he had the skill to deal with difficult customers – there were enough of them around – and with a graciousness barely spoilt by the gritting of his teeth he offered: 'I tell you what, sir. This wine I have, special, this is a discovery my brother in Tarquinia make. Very extra. He send it to me to try on my best friends.'

He produced a bottle, drew the cork with a flourish, and poured half a glass, then stood back to await their approval.

Jemima stared at the glass. Max stared at it. With one accord they reached out and nudged it towards Cy.

'Go on. *You* taste it!'

# A Little Bit of Wildlife

Jemima was not a person to follow fads, and when snide remarks were made about her jogging, she would sharply retort that fashion did not come into it, but fitness did.

That morning, however, it needed all of the famous Jemima Shore will-power to get out of bed the half hour early to do her stint through Holland Park. It was one of those miserable grey spring days that catch everybody out. At the first sign of spring and warmth, the British seem to go mad and declare the arrival of summer, only to face snow the following week. Jemima had not gone that far, but lying back in her bed contemplating the grey sky showing through her antique-lace curtains, she wondered whether her new regime was such a good idea. Jemima had no need to diet to keep her slim figure, and jogging was merely part of her new keep-fit regime to tone her up. She wondered whether it could also be attributed to spring madness.

However, she had given Cherry such a long lecture the previous day on the importance of looking after one's body that twinges of guilt finally pushed Jemima out of bed. She deftly brushed her hair back off her face and into a ponytail and climbed into one of the several tracksuits she had bought as an incentive to keep to her new regime. Real coffee — as always, none of the instant sort — was something to look forward to on her return from the park.

She was beginning to wake up. She bounced happily down all the stairs from her top-floor flat. She pulled the street door shut, and put the keys into the pocket of her velour top, and jogged off towards the park, checking the time on the sports watch she had originally bought to time scripts because of the stop-watch facilities. It was seven o'clock. She grimaced and looked up at the sky. It looked as if rain would not hold off for long, so she set off with extra vigour.

She entered the park through the Holland Park side entrance and turned up along the almost country-like paths, which are bounded by a wooden picket fence and thick shrubbery on either side. The park was deserted except for a small boy exercising his black labrador before going to school. 'Morning,' called Jemima, as she overtook the two of them. 'Hello,' the boy replied automatically — and then suddenly his eyes widened as he recognised Jemima Shore Investigator, television star.

By this time, Jemima had jogged on to the duck-pond. She slowed down for a moment to quack at the ducks, who took this greeting with ill grace and waddled off into the water, and then set off down an avenue of trees. There was a grassy area with a long park bench set well back from the path. Lying stretched out, full length on the bench, was a man with a check jacket draped over his head. Jemima jogged out of the wooded part of the park and up on to the grass that stretches off down to Kensington High Street. She stopped to take in the view and pause for breath. She was beginning to feel puffed, and looked at her watch. It was time to turn round so that she would be in good time for work. Moving more slowly, Jemima retraced her steps.

Mentally she went through her work schedule for the day – it was a quiet day with no meetings or interviews planned. All she had to do was think up a topic for the show in three weeks' time. Her somewhat flippant suggestion of an investigation into weekend holidays abroad had met with a stoney response from Cy, her programme controller. She *knew* she was right: the series needed some lightness injected into it. A solid diet of worthiness needed some leavening with the lighter side of life, she thought, as she panted back up the avenue of trees. Her thoughts were interrupted as she noticed out of the corner of her eye, the checked jacket lying in a heap on the ground by the park bench. The bench was empty; the owner of the jacket seemed to have disappeared. Jemima noticed a man walking away from her up the path, and assumed that the jacket belonged to him.

'Oi!', she called out, but the man continued on his way.

'Damn and blast,' Jemima muttered, stepping off the path and over to the seat. There she bent down and picked up the jacket. Summoning all her energy, she set off up the hill after the man, who was fast disappearing out of sight.

'I say!' panted Jemima, as she reached the man, who finally stopped and turned round to face her. He was a nondescript-looking man in his late thirties, broadly built, but below average height. He was dressed entirely in black. The only distinguishing feature was a bald patch on the top of his head.

'You left your jacket.' Jemima held out the garment to him.

'Not mine duckie!' the man said, looking Jemima up and down. He had a very, very slight accent. 'Not my style really.'

'No. No, of course it isn't.'

'What do you mean by that?' the man snapped.

This was useless, Jemima thought. 'Nothing. I'm sorry.'

'Haven't we met somewhere before? Your face seems familiar.'

'No, we haven't met.' Jemima was accustomed to her face being public property, but she didn't want to get into all that at this time in the morning.

'Put the jacket back where you found it, duckie. I must fly now or be late for work,' and with that response he hurried off.

Jemima turned back towards the bench, and to her dismay saw two punk rockers sitting on it. They were not a prepossessing sight, wearing tight plastic leather trousers, grubby T-shirts and hair highly brilliantined up into coxcombs. They seemed intent on inspecting their outsize Dr Marten's boots stretched out in front of them, but then one of the boys looked up and noticed Jemima. She felt she couldn't leave the jacket with them, so slung the coat over her shoulder and jogged off home.

Jemima had had a quick bath before changing into her smart cream suit for work and was sitting at her kitchen table with a cup of coffee engrossed in the *Guardian*, when Mrs B, her cleaning lady, bustled in. Mrs B's eyes missed nothing, and she immediately spotted the jacket from the park, which Jemima had hung over the back of a kitchen chair.

'Smart jacket. Haven't seen it before, have I? Belong to one of your young men?' Mrs B thought Jemima's private life should at least be public to her.

Jemima lowered the paper and looked across the table at Mrs B with exasperation. She could see that this jacket was going to prove a lot of bother.

'No, Mrs B. I actually found it lying by itself by a bench in the park.'

'Well, you should have left it where it was . . .'

'You're the second person to say that.' Jemima remarked bitterly.

Mrs B ploughed on. 'So whoever lost it would know where to find it.'

'I'm afraid it would have been stolen.'

'Well, that's right. It *has* been stolen, hasn't it,' re-joindered Mrs B who then asked Jemima, in a confiding manner, whether she had been through the pockets. That had been the first thing Jemima had done on getting home. She had hoped to trace the owner of the jacket, but all she found was a comb, handkerchief, and a book of matches from one of her favourite restaurants, L'Aubergine. The jacket was of good quality and cut, and probably French, but that was all the information Jemima could glean. She would drop it in at the police station on her way into work. However, determined to have the last word, Mrs B pointed out how late Jemima was, and so in fact she went directly to the office.

Cherry and she did a good morning's work clearing a backlog of letters. More importantly, she decided that she would do a programme about books – not a programme about hyping, pornography or the decline in literacy (although all that, no doubt, would come in to it) but a straightforward, self-indulgent revel in the world of books.

Cherry finished typing the last reply to Jemima's vast fan mail and was leaning back in her chair, complacently looking at her overflowing out tray. She was weighing up whether to upset Jemima by lighting up a cigarette or to put up with her pangs until lunch. Even before her keep-fit regime, Jemima was a firm non-smoker. Cherry decided to live dangerously and brought out her packet of cigarettes. Unfortunately, she had to draw attention to the fact, because she couldn't find her lighter. Leaving Cherry without any further doubts on her views on the pollution of the atmosphere, Jemima remembered the book of matches that she had found in the jacket. She went over to the coat rack, and tossed the matches across. As Cherry lit her cigarette, and was about to close the book, she noticed a name and number written on the inside flap.

'A new lover?' she inquired, nosily.

Jemima darted over to Cherry's desk and had a closer look at the book of matches. 'Mr Fox. 246 8091'. Impulsively, she asked Cherry to get the number, which turned out to be the Waldorf Hotel.

'Ask them if there's a Mr Fox staying there.' Jemima's hopes that she might be on the track of the owner of the jacket were dashed. Cherry shook her head. 'They've never heard of Mr Fox.' She replaced the receiver and looked curiously at Jemima, who was putting the matches back in the jacket.

'What's all this about. New jacket?'

'I'll tell you over lunch. I thought we might treat ourselves to lunch at L'Aubergine and ask if they know anything about the jacket.'

Near by her flat, L'Aubergine was one of Jemima's particular favourites. Sometimes when she was not in the mood for cooking she would go in and dine there on her own. One step up from a bistro, but not overly grand, L'Aubergine specialised in good quality, straightforward French cooking. It was a pretty place, filled with plants, painted dark green and white, and furnished in art-deco style. Each table had a thick cloth covering the wrought iron legs and was decorated with a small silver vase filled with fresh flowers.

'I think you should have left it where it was,' said Cherry, in response to Jemima's tale of the jacket.

Jemima put down her knife and fork on the plate. (It had taken until halfway through the main course for her to tell Cherry the saga.) 'If anyone else says that I'll scream. I behave as any decent citizen would, and all I get told is that I should have left well alone. It seemed a pity to make a present of it to a couple of punk rockers.'

'They wouldn't be seen dead in a jacket like that,' snorted Cherry. 'Why don't you just take it to the police station?'

Jemima explained patiently. 'In view of the matches, I thought Pierre might know who it belonged to.'

'It wouldn't be Mr Fox; that's for sure. You wouldn't write your own name and telephone number on a box of matches, would you?' Cherry interrupted.

'I'm well aware of that, my sleuthful Cherry. Still, Pierre might have some idea.' Jemima called Pierre, the head waiter, over to their table, but he had no recollection of the jacket or its owner, and neither did the name Mr Fox mean anything.

'Well and timely foxed, eh!' quipped Cherry. Then she looked at Jemima. 'Why are you so interested? It's only a boring old jacket.' Jemima shook her head. 'I don't really know. But I scent a mystery, perhaps.'

For the rest of the meal, the two women discussed the parlous state of Cherry's love life. They were finishing their coffee when Jemima's old friend, literary critic Jamie Grand, arrived in the restaurant. Noticing Jemima and Cherry, he made his way over to their table.

Jamie always reminded Jemima of Mother in *The Avengers*. Large, portly and avuncular, he always flirted outrageously with Jemima. Renowned in literary circles for his snappy dressing, Jamie was sporting a canary yellow waistcoat with his dark suit, matching carnation, white silk scarf, and cane.

Pierre laid a third place at the table for Jamie to join Jemima and Cherry. Cherry, however, had to go back to the office, and Jemima was not in the mood for exchanging witty banter with Jamie. The check jacket was beginning to niggle her intensely. Declining a glass of her favourite Sancerre, Jemima made to go, leaving Jamie alone with a succulent sole which had just been placed in front of him. Jemima prevented Pierre from helping her on with the check jacket, causing him to apologise. He handed the jacket over to Jemima, and as he opened the restaurant door for her to leave, he said, 'I hope you find your M'sieur Renard, Ma'm'selle Jemima.'

For a moment, Jemima was puzzled, and then laughed. 'Of course. "Fox" in French. Thank you, Pierre! 'Bye now.'

With that, she waved a final farewell to Jamie and left L'Aubergine, wondering if Pierre was correct in his deduction. There was one way to find out, and she set off down Westbourne Park Road, clutching the jacket, in search of a taxi.

The black cab dropped her off in the curve of the Aldwych, next to the Waldorf. She pushed her way through the revolving glass doors and walked up the steps to the reception desk. The entrance lobby was empty. There were no guests arriving or leaving. A couple of porters were hanging round the lifts, and the receptionist gave Jemima his immediate attention.

Pierre was right. A M. Renard had checked in only the previous evening and was somewhere in the hotel, his key being missing from the numbered pigeon hole. A porter was despatched to page M. Renard, and Jemima stood waiting, looking at the various portraits in the lobby.

After only a few minutes, the porter returned accompanied by a tall, dark, good-looking man of continental appearance, in his late thirties or early forties. Jemima queried:

'M'sieur Renard?'

'Oui, c'est moi.'

'Do you speak English?'

'Perfectly well.'

Jemima smiled, 'Good. My French has got a bit rusty.' In fact she could speak rather-better-than-schoolgirl French. 'My name is Jemima Shore, and we haven't met, but I'm . . .' Jemima was unexpectedly flustered by meeting M. Renard. She wasn't sure why – his undoubted good looks, a strange atmosphere coming from him. . . . There was something definitely different about him. Her hesitation was covered over by the approach of a young man who had been hovering. He asked for her autograph, and Jemima readily gave it, and one of her famous smiles as she handed back his autograph book.

Renard regarded her quizzically. 'You are famous? A film star perhaps?'

'No, nothing like that.' Jemima was surprised at how sharply she spoke. 'To get back to what I was saying; we haven't met, but I'm trying to trace the owner of this jacket.'

M. Renard fingered the jacket that Jemima held out. 'A very nice one. Has somebody lost it?'

'Yes, and I thought . . .'

'You thought it was me? That is most kind of you, but as you see, I have a jacket,' he laughed.

'Yes, but I thought you might know who it belongs to.' Renard looked inquiringly at Jemima. Fumbling with the jacket, Jemima extricated the book of matches and handed them over to Renard, explaining, 'There's the number of this hotel, and your name written on it.'

Renard glanced at the book, opened the flap and looked at the writing on the back of the cover. 'But my name is not Fox,' he murmured, in a slow, attractive continental accent, which Jemima couldn't quite place.

'It is in English,' she stated, simply. Renard grinned at her and burst into laughter. Feeling disconcerted, Jemima took back the matches and apologised. 'I obviously made a ridiculous mistake. I'm sorry to have troubled you.' She turned to leave the hotel, feeling embarrassed by the incident. A hand came down on her shoulder and she looked round. 'Wait a moment.' The tall Frenchman was smiling at her. 'Forgive me. I just found it rather funny. Why don't we go into the lounge and talk about it. We could have a cup of tea, perhaps?'

Regaining her composure, Jemima accepted his invitation. Afternoon tea with an attractive man was an unexpected treat on a grey spring day. 'I'm just about fed up with this wretched jacket – I should have taken it to the police station in the first place,' she explained, following him out of the reception area and across the hallway of the hotel.

'I am delighted you did not. Otherwise I would not have had the pleasure of meeting you,' said Renard as they strolled into the lounge. They stood in the entrance of the large airy room. Round the edge of the room were niches and marble columns. There was a large sunken area of yellow marble, with exotic palms and small tables and chairs. A palm court orchestra played to a small empty dance floor. The room was deserted except for a couple of tables with people taking tea.

Renard guided Jemima by the arm down the carpeted steps to a secluded table between two large palm trees, and ordered tea for two. Jemima smiled at him.

'I don't know what I'm doing here. I should be back at the office. Je suis fou.'

' "Folle",' he corrected her.

'Of course.' Jemima laughed. ' "Folle", feminine. I ought to know that.'

Renard gazed round the room, absorbing the surroundings.

'You know, I like this room. It's so romantic.' There was a moment of tension between them, broken by the arrival of the waiter with a tray laden with a full afternoon tea. 'Good Lord!' exclaimed Jemima, looking at the plates of sandwiches and cakes. 'I couldn't eat a cake. It's not that long since I had lunch.'

'It does not matter,' murmured Renard, as Jemima lifted the teapot.

'Shall I pour?' She gave him one of her long looks through her half-closed eyelashes. 'As a matter of fact, I had lunch where those matches come from – L'Aubergine. Do you know it?'

Renard paused for a moment, and then asked, 'It is in West 11, isn't it?'

'That's right. Milk?' Jemima glanced up at him.

Renard shook his head. 'No, thank you. I'll have a slice of lemon. Yes, I have been to L'Aubergine but, y'know, in England I prefer to eat your roast beef, your fish and chips . . .'

Jemima sipped her tea and started to relax. They started to make the exploratory sort of conversation that people do make when they first get to know each other. She was rather attracted by this mysterious foreigner. He lived in Paris but did not come from there. He said he was an *homme d'affaires*, a business consultant advising English people wanting to invest in French businesses. He was intrigued how Jemima had found the jacket and tracked him down. Was there nothing in the jacket apart from the book of matches to identify the owner? When Renard became the fourth person that day to suggest to

Jemima that she took the jacket to the police, she showed her exasperation.

'I can assure you, I'm going right there when I leave here. The whole thing's turned out to be a dratted nuisance.'

'Am I a dratted nuisance?' Renard looked at her reproachfully.

'No, that's not at all what I meant,' smiled Jemima.

'In that case,' Renard leant across the table, 'may I be permitted to ask you to dance?' Still smiling, Jemima rose from the table and followed Renard across to the tiny dance floor. Renard drew her close to him and she was pleased to find that he was an excellent dancer. He was also unusually tall, and Jemima only just came up to his shoulders. She looked up into his twinkling dark brown eyes and said, 'I've never danced with a French fox before.'

'And what do you think?' He eased her closer to him.

'I think he's a remarkably good dancer. He is also a very charming fellow.'

'Very sly, with remarkably sharp teeth,' he teased, looking down at Jemima. He bared his teeth slightly causing Jemima to laugh.

'Is that a fact? Never mind. I like to live dangerously.' As they gracefully moved over the dance floor, Jemima was not to know what an ironic statement that was.

Back at Megalith Television, Cherry had dealt with all the routine paperwork and was staving off the numerous people who were clamouring for Jemima. Jemima had rung in, saying she would be out for the afternoon, and they arranged to meet at the end of the day at Megalith's local wine bar, Tasha's.

At six o'clock, Cherry was perched on a stool at the bar there. It was a glossy chic cocktail bar furnished with a chrome-and-glass bar and large comfortable sofas, covered in the latest fashionable acid pink and green colours. Cherry was wondering what latest adventure Jemima had stumbled into. Her employer had an extraordinary knack of getting involved in bizarre and exciting happenings, mused Cherry, sipping her glass of wine. Suddenly, she heard a voice demanding, 'Where *is* Jemima?' It was Lady Miranda, one of Jemima's oldest women friends. They had both been at the same convent school together. These days, Miranda's husband concentrated on horse-breeding in the country while Miranda looked after her string of exclusive dress shops. Cherry knew Miranda from the times she had gone to her main shop with Jemima in search of outfits for Jemima to wear in the show. Those afternoons when the two of them went off shopping on Megalith's money always felt to Cherry as if they were playing truant, and so had a special spicy charm.

'I haven't seen her since lunch,' answered Cherry, as Miranda eased herself onto a stool next to Cherry, and then ordered each of them a glass of white wine. She was holding forth so strongly and loudly on the unreliability of the flibberty-gibbet girls she had in her shop that Cherry was glad when Jemima entered the wine bar looking flushed and happy, and without the jacket.

'You look positively glowing,' remarked Miranda, as the women moved from the bar and sat themselves more comfortably in the corner, on two shiny pink sofas round a low table. Jemima failed to follow up this remark and inquired about Miranda's home life, but finally she could not escape from the sort of nosiness admissable only after years of friendship. She had to admit that she had spent the afternoon at a tea dance at the Waldorf with a very charming Frenchman. Feeling satisfied that she had gained some gossip, Miranda suddenly decided to leave and bustled out. Cherry had worked with Jemima long enough not to accept her simple explanation of anything. Sensing something was being held back, she looked at her boss with interest.

'So tell me, Jemima Shore Investigator: what were you doing before you came here?'

'Nothing very interesting. I took that lost jacket to the police station, where a rather bored PC took my name and address.'

'I'm talking about the hotel,' interrupted Cherry.

'Oh,' Jemima smiled. 'I was Fox-hunting.'

Cherry looked surprised. 'But he wasn't there?'

'Oh, but he was! I flushed him out,' said Jemima, triumphantly.

There was a slight pause for Cherry to assimilate this information, and then she inclined her head and asked, 'A French Fox?' A mysterious smile passed across Jemima's face. 'Exactement. Let's have another drink, shall we?' And with that, Cherry had to be satisfied. She knew she could get no further by any more probing and that she would have to wait to find out anything more about Jemima's 'Fench Fox'. A following half hour was spent with Cherry filling in Jemima about what she had missed that afternoon, and then they both went home.

After the gluttonies of the day before, Jemima had no difficulty of resolve in getting up early the following day to follow her jogging regime. By now, she had established a standard route to follow. The same small boy was there again in the park exercising his black labrador. They waved as Jemima jogged past, and this time he plucked up his courage and ran after her for her autograph. First refusing, then noticing how crestfallen he looked, Jemima promised to give it to him on her way back if he was still around. The small boy seemed pleased with that, and ran off with his dog.

Jemima jogged on down the avenue of trees towards

the entrance into Kensington High Street. She felt pleased with herself: she was feeling much less puffed than she had yesterday, although the muscles in the back of her calves were aching. It was time to turn round, otherwise she was going to be late into work again. The exercise was beginning to tell as she came back up the hill, up along to the avenue of trees. She was just beginning to regret her premature complacency and having to slow down when the small boy suddenly appeared in front of her, blocking her path, and giving her the perfect excuse to stop. As she held her hand out for his autograph book, she noticed he was very upset. Close to tears, he told her that he had lost his dog, George – the black labrador. About to scold him for letting him off the lead and so disturbing the park's wildlife, Jemima couldn't help but feel sorry for the unhappy boy. Together they walked up the avenue towards the Holland Park end, Jemima whistling for the dog, and the small boy calling him by name. They had just passed the spot where Jemima had found the jacket the day before when they heard a sniffing sound coming from the dense shrubbery. They stopped and saw the labrador's black tail waving furiously in the air from the undergrowth. The small boy rushed across the grass, over the broken-down fence, and plunged into the shrubbery, pushing aside the thick foliage. The dog was worrying at something, giving out little growls and becoming increasingly excited. Jemima walked up to the fence and watched as George scrabbled back out of the shrubbery, with a man's black shoe in his mouth. Smacking the dog, the boy leant down to pick up the dog's lead. As he bent down he saw a pair of men's feet, with only one shoe on, sticking out from the bushes. He gasped and pulled the dog back by the lead, out over the fence. 'Stand back a minute,' said Jemima. Parting the bushes, Jemima saw a man lying stretched out on his back on the earth. He was clearly dead. Flies were buzzing round him, his eyes bulging out of his head and his tongue hanging out of the side of his mouth, a purple-blue. Quickly, Jemima let the branches drop and swallowed hard. She paused for a moment to compose herself, and then turned to the boy. Leading him by the hand, she went to sit down on the nearby bench. The small boy's delight in finding his dog was overpowered by what he had discovered, and he was feeling rather frightened. In an attempt to soothe him, Jemima asked him his name, and for his autograph book. Still holding George by the lead with one hand, Michael extricated his book and Biro from his blazer pocket, and handed them over to Jemima. She opened the book and signed her signature with a flourish. Michael was visibly recovering, and waited for Jemima to return the book.

'Now, I want you to do something for me,' Jemima asked and tore a fresh page out of his autograph book. She then wrote down a telephone number, folded the piece of paper in half, and handed it and the book back to Michael.

'I want you to go home and call this number. Ask for Superintendent Tree, and ask him to come straight away. To exactly where I am now. Will you do that?' Michael nodded and, looking towards the shrubbery, asked, 'Miss Shore, that man in there, is he very ill?'

Jemima looked up at him and gravely answered, 'Yes, Michael, I'm afraid he is.'

'Right. 'Byee,' said Michael, suddenly cheerful. He leapt up from the bench, tugged on the lead, and he and George dashed off out of the park.

Jemima remained seated on the bench, staring out straight in front of her. Her thoughts were grim. She felt certain that the dead man was the same one as had been lying on the bench yesterday, and that the jacket she had been trailing around belonged to the dead man. Where did the mysterious M. Renard fit in, if indeed he did?

Later that day, Jemima was ensconced (over another pot of tea) in Det. Chief Supt Tree's office. Jemima Shore Investigator had excellent relations with the Met. – although she would occasionally joke that her pro-gramme should really turn its eagle eye on the murkier workings of the police force.

By matching hairs, the Police Forensic Department had confirmed what Jemima had suspected, that the jacket that she had picked up the previous day did belong to the dead man.

The dead man had also definitely been murdered – garrotted. As Jemima said, she didn't think a man could have strangled himself. The Police Surgeon had esti-mated the body to have been dead for twenty-four hours when Jemima discovered it. So, as Tree took her through her movements in the park, the more anxious Jemima became that she must have unconsciously seen the mur-derer, and that the person she had noticed lying on the bench covered with the jacket might have been dead at the time.

Who could it have been? The small boy Michael was beyond suspicion. It seemed highly unlikely that the punk rockers had been the murderers. They would not have hung round at the site of the crime. She could not even recall the man whom she had initially thought owned the jacket as being there when she first jogged past the bench. But the murderer must have been in the vicinity.

That was easily explained, said Tree. Having garrotted his victim, the murderer, hearing Jemima approach on her early-morning jog, would have pushed his victim down on the bench, covered over with the jacket, whilst he – the murderer – hid in the bushes until she had passed by. Tree hoped that the other people, those she had seen, would come forward when they read about the affair in the newspapers, and that he would issue descriptions of all the individuals. There was really very little to go on. The identity of the man was completely mysterious. Nothing had been found on the body to give any clue of whom he might be. Jemima had replaced the book of matches in the jacket and wondered what the police had made of them. Having given the police all the direct assistance she could, Jemima decided to keep the meeting with Renard to herself. She told Tree that she had phoned the hotel in search of a Mr Fox, but she did not tell him about M. Renard. The prosaic Tree would consider the link between Fox and Renard as fanciful whimsy. Jemima hoped that it was coincidence that a M. Renard was staying at the Waldorf at the same time as she had been trying to trace a Mr Fox there – she would find out later that evening, for she had invited him round to dinner to sample some good home-made English food at her flat. If he was in any way implicated with the dead man, then surely he would not turn up? If that happened, she would have to tell the police about the French Fox, but in the meantime she would let them get on with the investigation. However, Jemima did give the police a piece of information which would help them with their inquiries: L'Aubergine had changed its match-book cover only the other week.

By the time she had left Supt Tree, Jemima was already late for her recce at Mr Mueller's bookshop. She had arranged to meet Cherry there in order to do some background field research for her programme on books. She wasn't sure what angle it would take as yet, but that was the reason why she often did her own research and did not rely solely on her team of research assistants. She frequently found that it was while she was chatting to her interviewees that she thought of an unusual or more interesting approach to a subject. Jemima loved books and was great friends with several second-hand bookshop owners across London.

On her arrival at the shop, Mr Mueller directed Jemima downstairs, where Cherry was busy chatting to people browsing along the shelves. She had just finished talking to a man who claimed to like thrillers, preferably 'murders', when Jemima climbed down the rickety stairs to the dark, crowded basement. The man had turned away from Cherry and brushed past Jemima at the foot of the stairs and hurried up off out of the shop. Jemima froze for a moment, and then ordered Cherry to follow the man and to meet her back at the office later.

Was this another strange coincidence? There had been no mistaking the man: he was the same one as she had thought had owned the jacket in the park. Jemima's uncanny intuition was alerted, but about what, she wasn't yet sure. However, she felt she was being drawn into something rather mysterious.

The man from the park was not known to Mr Mueller, and Jemima continued to work through the afternoon as previously planned. She spoke to a number of people coming into Mr Mueller's shop and then went back to Megalithic House.

Seeking refuge from the telephone, Jemima went to the wine bar to wait for Cherry. As well as all the work calls, Jemima had been bombarded with people ringing up wanting to hear how exactly she had found the dead body. The news of her discovery had been the front-page story in the lunchtime edition of the evening paper. 'Grissly find by TV Investigator in Park,' ran the headline. (Jemima was relieved to see that it had been replaced by the state of the pound and moved inside in later editions.)

It had gone half-past six, and Cherry hadn't turned up. Jemima was beginning to worry lest something had happened to her – had she sent her assistant off on a dangerous mission? But at that moment, a rather tired and flustered Cherry arrived in the wine bar. Flopping down on the sofa next to Jemima, Cherry stretched out her legs and grasped the glass of wine that Jemima pushed towards her.

'Drink.'

'Thanks.' Cherry picked up the paper that Jemima had been reading and started reading the piece about the body in the park.

'Come on, don't keep me in suspense.' Jemima's relief at Cherry's safe arrival was now displaced by her curiosity to know what had taken her so long. Cherry crossed her legs and looked nonchalant.

'No suspense about it really. I followed the individual in question – and very boring it was too.'

'Did he notice you?'

'I don't think so. Anyway, I don't think it would have mattered much if he had.'

'Go on,' urged Jemima.

Cherry rolled her eyes upwards indicating an afternoon of utter boredom. 'Well, he walked, and I walked. He went for a work-out in a gym in High Street Ken while yours truly kicked her heels on the pavement outside. Finally, he comes out, buys a copy of the *Standard* and sits down to read it in a rather nasty coffee bar. Then he leaves and I leave, and we end up at the police station.'

'The police station?' asked Jemima.

'Yes, that's what I said. He went in, right up the steps, right through the glass doors, and inside. I saw him talking to the man at the desk. Who is he anyway?'

Baffled by what Cherry had told her, Jemima decided to go and give Supt Tree a ring. Could he fill her in any more? She left Cherry sipping her wine and reading the *Standard*. Cherry had finished the paper and nearly all the bottle of wine by the time Jemima returned. It wasn't that Tree had been unhelpful – in fact, he told Jemima all he knew. It just didn't get them very far. The man Cherry followed had been the same one as she had talked to in the park, and reading about the murder in the paper he decided he had better go and see the police. His name was Mickey Martin and he walked through the park every day to work. The punks had also offered to help the police and they had seen nothing either.

Cherry assimilated all this information. 'So this leaves us with person or persons unknown, doesn't it?' Jemima nodded. Cherry paused for a moment and, looking straight at Jemima, asked her, 'Did you mention M. Renard to Supt Tree?'

Trying to look disingenuous, Jemima admitted that she hadn't mentioned him, and anyway why should she.

Cherry shook her head, 'I don't know Jem. But you did say you thought it was odd.' Jemima smiled at her assistant. She was amused by Cherry's reactions, a mixture of concern for her boss of whom she was very fond, and a desire to get mixed up in one of Jemima's adventures.

'Life is full of little coincidences that don't really mean anything,' said Jemima, trying to set Cherry's mind at ease.

'But what if he *were* somehow suspect?' persisted Cherry.

'In that case, he most certainly won't show up for dinner, will he?'

'So, you're having dinner with the French Fox?' Cherry was intrigued. Life somehow wasn't fair; Jemima always seemed to have such an exciting time.

'No, the French Fox is having dinner with me –' Jemima looked at her watch – 'which means I had better get my skates on.'

She stood up from the sofa and bent down to pick up the plastic shopping bags that contained the ingredients of the meal she would cook that night.

'What are you cooking?' Cherry's interest was not polite good manners but genuine interest. Spending the previous summer holidays gaining a cordon-bleu diploma for herself in Paris had been no casual pastime.

'Steak and kidney pie.'

'Terrific. He *must* be very attractive.'

'He is. *Il est ravissant.* 'Bye now.'

Weighed down by her shopping, Jemima left the wine bar and rushed home. It was now gone seven, and her guest was due at eight-thirty. It was going to be a tight scramble to prepare the food, have a bath and change to be ready and relaxed for his arrival. But at least the traffic had cleared by that time, and she made the drive from Megalithic House to her flat in good time.

Jemima was a good cook herself and had made steak and kidney pie many times for foreign guests. It always seemed to impress them. She went into a state of semi-automatic pilot as she made the pastry in her food processor and cooked the filling.

Her kitchen was a large one for a one-bedroomed flat. She had knocked out the wall between the kitchen and her living room so she could chat to her guests if she was cooking. It was well fitted, with plenty of work surfaces; the units were pine and her pride and joy, the specially installed Aga, was both cooker and hot water boiler. The wall on which the Aga was positioned had been taken back to the original brick and hung with momentoes such as the large copper 'J' that a former lover had given her. In the centre of the room was a large scrubbed pine table which served as both kitchen and dining table.

Having cooked the main dish so many times, she had no need of a cookery book. She dashed through the preparations in record time. The starter of smoked eel, bought from her favourite delicatessen, needed no cooking. White wine was cooling in the fridge. A methodical person, Jemima washed up as she went along and so had little to clear up before she laid the table. She need not have worried – everything was ready in plenty of time to have a bath and change.

Jemima was lying back on her sofa, doting on *Don Giovanni*, one of her most-loved operas, when the doorbell rang. She opened the front door to Renard. He stood there looking as handsome as she had remembered, holding a brief case in one hand and a wrapped bottle in the other. He came into the flat and gave Jemima the bottle as she took his coat. 'For you, Ma'm'selle.'

'Thank you very much.' She unwrapped the bottle of Quern and gasped appreciatively. She looked at his brief case. 'I see you came from work.' He smiled, and put it down in the hall before following Jemima through into the sitting room.

He glanced round the room. 'I know a lot about you already; you have a very charming apartment, you like Mozart.' He raised the glass of whisky and soda to Jemima, and she sipped the white wine that she always drank. 'How is your hotel?' she asked, indicating that he sit on the sofa; she was positioned in a chair nearer the kitchen.

'The same.'

'How long will you stay there?'

212

Renard shrugged his shoulders, 'I don't know exactly. It depends on my business.' They both sat in silence, enjoying the music. The atmosphere grew warm and relaxed. Renard broke it with: 'If you come to Paris, you must come to the Opera with me.'

'You're not married then, Renard?'

'To my work, like you are.'

Jemima laughed. 'You can say that again. I must see to things in the kitchen; you stay here and look at the paper.' She handed him the *Standard*.

'I have seen it. I bought the early edition. I saw your photograph and read about the body you discovered. It must have been a shock for you.'

'It was. Especially at that time of the morning.' Jemima handed Renard a bottle of wine to open and went in the kitchen to look at the pie.

Dinner was a great success, with Renard complimenting Jemima on a *formidable* steak and kidney pie. They exchanged musical anecdotes, but part of the meal was spent discussing Jemima's discovery of the dead body. The dead man's jacket brought them together. Renard was interested to know if the body had been identified, and whom the police suspected. Jemima laughingly said that all the suspects had gone to the police: herself, the punk rockers and Mickey Martin.

The meal was over and they were sitting over coffee and glasses of Quern when Renard rose up from his seat and wandered across to her window. 'What was this Mickey Martin like?'

Jemima described him. 'Why do you ask?'

'Just curiosity. Was he English?'

She rose to join him. 'Well, he didn't look it actually, but apart from his speech I'd say he'd been here some time.' She picked up the bottle of Quern. 'Drink?' She filled up his glass, and they stood together looking out of the window in silence. Jemima sensed a change in the relaxed atmosphere between them and looked at him anxiously. The tension was broken by the phone ringing.

Jemima left the window and crossed the room. She picked up the receiver to hear Cherry fretting about her. Feeling concern for her boss's well-being, Cherry had rung the Waldorf and found out that Renard had checked out that afternoon. Would Jemima please call Supt Tree? Jemima's natural irritation at the interruption of her evening was lessened by the fact that Cherry had added to her own increasing feeling of unease with Renard. Reassuring Cherry that she would ring the police, Jemima replaced the receiver and left the sitting room to go to her bedroom.

She was sitting on her pretty brass bed covered in a Victorian white lace bedspread when she heard the key turn in the lock.

'Do not call anyone, Jemima.' Renard was standing by the door, putting down a tray holding two wine glasses. Enraged, Jemima leapt off the bed, dropping the phone as she did so.

'How dare you! Give me the key at once.'

She threw herself at him like a tigress. But without too much effort, Renard grabbed both her wrists and held them in a vice-like grip. He then lifted her slim body up and threw her back on the bed. He picked the telephone from the floor, and placed it as far away from the bed as the wire would stretch, with the receiver off the hook.

He walked back and sat on the bed.

'I will put the key back, but I would like you to listen to a little *histoire* first. Will you listen?'

Jemima was livid. 'I don't seem to have much choice in the matter. But since you've brought my drink in here, perhaps you'd give it to me, please.'

Renard rose, fetched both the drinks, and resumed sitting on the bed. He took a photograph from his wallet and handed it to Jemima.

'It is about the body you found in the park. Was this the victim?'

Jemima gulped the wine and took the photograph. She recognised the face. 'Yes. Yes, I would say that it was.' She looked hard at Renard, returning the photo. Renard replaced it in the wallet and explained.

'He was a friend, someone I worked with. It was his jacket you brought to the hotel yesterday.'

Jemima leant forward, her anger being replaced by curiosity. 'So why on earth didn't you say so?'

'Because, until this afternoon, I didn't know what had happened to him. I suspected of course, when he did not call me as arranged.'

Jemima sighed, 'So "Fox" did mean "Renard".'

'Absolutely.'

'So, do you know who killed your friend?'

'I know very well.'

Excitedly, Jemima burst out, 'It was the man I described to you, wasn't it? Mickey Martin, the man I saw in the park. Then why don't you go to the police?'

Renard shook his head, 'I do not wish to be involved.'

'But you *are* involved,' retorted Jemima. 'It's *your* friend who's been murdered. Do you know why?'

By this time Jemima was sitting crossed legged up by her pillows as Renard leant back against the end of the bed. He explained how neither he nor his friend was French. They were dissidents in exile, and his friend wrote articles of a nature subversive to the present regime. The articles were distributed in their homeland. He had been found out, and so disposed of.

Jemima believed him, and felt she was no longer under

threat; she got up from the bed and replaced the telephone receiver. 'I'm not going to call anyone.' She paced the room and stopped. 'Renard, you *must* go to the police. You *must* tell them who the victim is and who killed him.'

Renard shook his head again. 'No, Jemima. It is not important that the police know. *I* know. That's what matters.' He finished his drink and continued. 'Eventually, of course, the police will find out. It will take some time. My friend lived in a small anonymous flat, like a small, anonymous, grey monk. His luck ran out.'

'What about *your* luck?' asked Jemima, with concern as well as irony.

Renard struggled. 'I am something of a fatalist, you know.' Jemima picked up her glass, finished her drink, and sat down next to Renard.

'So you will go back to France, Renard? Of course that can't possibly be your name, any more than Fox is.'

'It suffices, and I have grown fond of it. Especially when you say it.' Jemima gave him a sharp look. 'I must go back to France. I leave tomorrow morning.' She rose from the bed.

'And where are you staying tonight. Don't say the Waldorf, because I know better.'

Renard smiled. 'Of course you do, Madame Investigator!' He got up from the bed and moved across to Jemima. 'With you, Jemima.' She moved quickly away. 'I see,' she said. 'Well, the cards seem to be stacked in your favour, don't they? The bedroom key in your pocket . . .' She reached the bed quickly, stripping off and leaping under the bedclothes. She lay there on her back with her arms over the sheet firmly pulled up to her neck. She watched Renard headily.

He looked at Jemima and removed the key from his pocket and unlocked the bedroom door.

'Voilà, the choice is yours.'

Jemima sat up slightly, surprised. 'You trust me?' Renard walked back to the bed and sat on it. 'But, of course, if you give me any trouble I shall kill you.'

Jemima leant back into the pillows and looked at him from under her eyelashes. 'I'm far too sleepy to give you any trouble, Renard. Make yourself at home on the sofa.'

He stretched over and put his hand gently on her shoulder and stroked her arm.

'I would rather make myself at home in your bed,' he murmured.

The original attraction, there at their first meeting, had been returning, even during their strange conversation, and Jemima turned her head towards him, smiled, and said, 'In that case, why don't you kiss me, French Fox?' Renard leant over her and took her in his arms . . .

The following morning, Jemima woke late to find herself alone in bed. She felt a slight headache, and picked up the empty wine glass to sniff it. A small note was propped up beside her bedside lamp. She reached out and picked it up; it read, 'If you come sometime to Paris, take a coffee at "Le Crisbie" on St Germain. I will find you.' It was signed with a drawing of a fox. She sighed, and got out of bed and into her jogging suit. An immediate return to her regular regime was in order.

Forlornly, she jogged through the park, following her usual route. She was musing on all that Renard had told her the previous night when a young police constable stopped her. The rest of the park was cordoned off. However, using the famous Jemima Shore charm, and her connections with Supt Tree, she was allowed through. She jogged on to the area where, the constable said, the accident had occurred.

Supt Tree was standing by the duck-pond, watching police, in waders, drag a body out of the water. Jemima jogged up to Tree and stood next to him as the drowned man was placed on a police stretcher. Jemima started with recognition. The body was of a man in his mid-thirties, stockily built, with a tonsure.

'Recognise him?' Tree asked Jemima. She nodded.

'Mickey Martin.'

'Broken neck,' Tree told Jemima, as they walked away from the pond and the attendant police, and down the avenue of trees to the other murder spot. The Superintendent was postulating various motives for the murders: he assumed they were linked. Jemima volunteered 'retribution' as a possible explanation, but he only laughed: 'A vendetta, perhaps.'

Jemima felt that the circle had been completed. She had no further wish to talk to the policeman. She was going to keep her knowledge to herself.

'I don't think I'm going to be a lot of help to you,' she said, 'on this one.'

'Never mind, my dear. Truth will out eventually. These cases can't be solved in a hurry.'

Jemima looked at Tree. 'Do you speak French, Superintendent?'

'After a fashion: "La plume de ma tante" – that sort of thing,' he answered. 'Why do you ask?'

Jemima smiled enigmatically, 'Just wondered,' and jogged off.

The events of the past three days upset Jemima more than she would admit to anybody. All morning, she found her mind wandering back to Renard and what the truth really was. Witnessing two murdered corpses and having been held a virtual prisoner in one's own bedroom with an attractive, if lethal, man was more excitement than even Jemima Shore Investigator dealt with on a daily basis. Momentarily, her equilibrium had been knocked and although she knew she could soon regain her poise, she left the office to have an early lunch on her own.

Instinctively, she made her way to L'Aubergine. Pierre's inquiry if she had found her Mr Fox almost drove her away, but she decided to stay, and sat down in a discreet corner. She was halfway through her salmon trout and salad when dear old Jamie Grand showed up. Her tetchiness began to ebb away as Jamie sat down and commiserated her on the 'macabre happenings in the park'. She poured him the last of her wine and said, 'There was another one this morning in the park.'

'Really!' Jamie exclaimed. 'An escaped lunatic, perhaps?'

'No,' Jemima shook her head. 'Nothing random. All carefully thought out.'

'Political?' asked Jamie. Jemima nodded her head. 'Oh, I see. And are we looking for one murderer or two?' Jemima knew Jamie well enough not to be surprised by his shrewdness. 'That is a good question Jamie ... and I'm afraid we don't know the answer. One man murders another in the park and then gets murdered himself by a third man. "Good," we say ... poetic justice! And what better if the third man, who's a delightful fellow, gets away with it. Nice romantic ending?'

Jamie looked quizzically at Jemima. She continued.

'But ... suppose the third man isn't quite as delightful as he seems? Suppose he did *both* the murders. What then?'

'An interesting *dénouement* of course, but not quite so pleasant. Which theory do you favour, my dear?'

Jemima gazed briefly into her glass of wine, and then looked up. 'Oh, the first one of course. I might look like a tough nut Jamie, but I'm really very romantic.'

'That is one of the reasons I find you so bewitching.' Jamie leant over the table and stroked her arm. 'I think we'll share another bottle of your favourite Sancerre, don't you?'

Jemima laughed. 'The only thing is, I have this sudden mad impulse to catch a plane to Paris. What do you think?'

'Ah, one should never resist one's impulses my dear. A trip to Paris would be good for you. Take your mind off murder,' Jamie said regretfully.

Picking up her glass, Jemima said, 'You know Jamie, you could just be wrong about that. Cheers!' She raised her glass and drank. 'Vive la France!'